Redshifted: Martian Stories

Third Flatiron Anthologies
Volume 2, Winter 2013

Edited by Juliana Rew
Cover Art by Keely Rew

Dedication

For all of us who ever dreamed of one day setting foot on Mars. This anthology is dedicated to all the fine scientists, many located in Boulder, who continue to explore the Red Planet, albeit via unmanned satellites and remotely controlled rovers. May the Curiosity, MAVEN, and future missions continue to make more astonishing discoveries.

Redshifted: Martian Stories
Third Flatiron Anthologies
Volume 2, Winter 2013

Published by Third Flatiron Publishing
Juliana Rew, Editor

Copyright 2013 Third Flatiron Publishing
ISBN #9780615926186

Discover other titles by Third Flatiron:
(1) Over the Brink: Tales of Environmental Disaster

(2) A High Shrill Thump: War Stories

(3) Origins: Colliding Causalities

(4) Universe Horribilis

(5) Playing with Fire

(6) Lost Worlds, Retraced

Contents

*****～～～～*****

Eurydice in Capricorn

by Neil James Hudson

Eurydice in Aries

The start of the cycle. This is a good time to start any project that contributes to colonising the new world, and abandoning the old one.

...

Officially it's called Dome One, but we all call it Bradbury City and to hell with the bureaucrats. Everybody has a copy of *The Martian Chronicles*. In fact, there is only one book which exists in more copies, and that is *Martian Astrology* by Jasper Brett. I am not proud.

Of course I don't believe a word of it. Nobody does, certainly not the clients who come to me for readings or who avidly study my pages as if they contain some genuine wisdom. As one of my regular clients puts it, "Of course I don't believe it. But that doesn't stop it being true."

Her name is Kara. She works in communications and tells me as little as I tell her. I get my tablet to plot the positions of the various celestial bodies both now and when she arrived on this world, but I come up with the readings myself, feeling that I wouldn't be giving value for money if I got a program to do it. I pretend to know her real self, and she pretends to be surprised. But I appreciate her company, and always look forward to our meetings. I sometimes even think we might have made a good couple, if—

But I don't know what if.

...

Eurydice in Taurus

Persistence is the watchword here, even to the point of stubbornness. Doubts must be overcome, even persistent and stubborn ones.

...

I invented Martian astrology, because if I hadn't, someone else would have done, and I could do it better. There were few changes. Firstly, Mars is out of the picture. You're standing on it, so its movements are irrelevant. Instead, you have Earth, passing through the constellations. It represents what is precious, what you would fight for, what we have lost.

Earth's moon doesn't count, but Phobos and Deimos are major players. I decided that Phobos was easy enough, representing our fears. Deimos, then, was a counter, our hopes. Deimos is physically smaller, but on my charts they are the same size, balancing each other. Phobos is rising now.

At that same reading, Kara asked me about this. "It's not for me, it's for other people," I said. "I did a reading for the President once. He didn't believe it either, but he encouraged me. He said it gave people some meaning in their lives, some sense of purpose—the one thing we desperately need."

"But is there no part of it you believe?" said Kara, hunting in her pocket for a worthless currency to pay me in.

"There is one part I believe," I said. "But that's just for me."

"Tell me," she said.

...

Eurydice in Gemini

No point trying to be decisive. Much better to adapt to situations as they arrive, and rationalise your actions afterwards.

...

I led her outside. We walked to part of the dome that was transparent to the sky. I always believed that the air tasted artificial, but blind tests on Earth had never proven a difference. I looked up, and watched the small

8

light between Castor and Pollux, its movement imperceptible.

"You invented an astrology about Eurydice?"

"Why not? It's the most important thing in the sky."

We were silent for a few seconds, in which I imagined that the dome wasn't there and we were naked to the elements.

"Do you think the names were ill-starred?"

"Yes, but what names aren't? Virtually everyone in classical mythology came to a sticky end. No one told those of us on Orpheus not to look back. Quite the opposite: we were supposed to eagerly anticipate Eurydice's arrival. Whatever happened, it was nothing to do with the myth."

"Did you have family on it?"

"I was aware of how much I was telling her that I had told no one before, but I also couldn't think of a reason to keep it secret. "We were married, but only on Earth. And I am not on Earth, and he is not on Mars."

Of course, she wanted me to ask about her story, rather than tell my own, but I suppose we're all self-obsessed here.

...

Eurydice in Cancer

This is time to consider those to whom you are loyal, and those for whom you care. And to work out who they are.

...

"Eurydice represents your other half," I said. "Literally. The part of you that is hidden not just from other people, but from yourself. The part with which you need to be reunited in order to become whole again."

Eurydice was larger than Orpheus. We were the advance party, joining with the eight people who had already landed, with just enough tools and materials to build a habitable settlement. Eurydice followed a year

9

behind, with far more materials and many more people, to turn our makeshift shanty town into a proper city.

When Jerrett and I had learnt that we would not be on the same ship, we nearly abandoned our dream altogether. We stayed up many nights talking, trying to weigh our desire—our need—to be married on Mars with the separation that it would entail. The trip took two years, which meant it would be three before we met again. We compared ourselves to Odysseus and Penelope, and decided that our love was strong enough to survive those three years.

Eurydice arrived in Mars orbit on schedule, three months ago, and at each of our readings, I would ask Kara the same question, "Any word from the ship?"

And each time she would reply, "You know there isn't."

...

Eurydice in Leo

At this stage, you will be at your most confident and ambitious. There is no point trying to avoid mistakes, as you will make them anyway.

...

I ran through the meanings I had devised for the positions of the ship in the sky.

"Publish it," said Kara.

"No, it was a private game."

"Seriously. You said this gives people meaning to their lives. Well, make that meaningful." She gestured to the point in the sky where the silent ship fell in its orbit.

"Okay," I found myself saying.

I felt guilty about adding to the trash that I'd already produced. But part of me felt pride. We were a new land, with no history or mythology of our own. I was writing the new lore. Did it have to be real? The original Orpheus wasn't. My work wasn't rubbish; it was a kind of a folk tale that might still be told in millennia.

Eurydice in Capricorn

I looked at my notes. They were brief, only two hundred words, and I knew I would have to expand them to book length. Perhaps I could work some stories in, create a new mythology. Perhaps I could make some vague predictions.

Eurydice's symbol on my charts was a capital H, representing its real shape. I had a quick look at its future movements, and laughed out loud. We were only two months away from an astrological event, a triad with Phobos and Earth. I could hang something on that, pretend something important would happen. At the least, it gave me a deadline.

And suddenly, I had the idea.

...

Eurydice in Virgo

Your analytical and logical side will come to the fore. You will realise, logically, that you are over-analysing, but only through self-analysis.

...

The worst thing about Eurydice is that we don't even know if its passengers are alive or dead. Even the mythological Orpheus had that knowledge. They entered our orbit as expected, then cut all communication. The landing craft never exited the ship. They made no maneouvre, not even any minor external repair. But there is no reason why they should have died.

I do not know which I would prefer. If Jerrett is up there, stranded, within sight of the planet where we were to marry, or if one day we will open the airlocks and discover the corpses, unburied and unmourned.

Earth has no answers: they, too, lost contact. And they refuse to send a relief ship until they know what happened, which they can't find out without sending a ship.

Sometimes, I ask myself how long I will wait before I can declare myself single again. I am sure that I won't move on until long after that, but when do I give up? It has already been over three years.

People often ask me if my charts show when something will happen—when they either land, or we can prove they are dead. My answers are always noncommittal.

Until today. The triad shows it. The triad means something will happen.

It doesn't, of course. How could it? But aren't our myths more important than our realities?

...

Eurydice in Libra

You are at your most diplomatic, managing situations rather than winning them. Always with a nagging doubt that you've made one compromise too far.

...

My meeting was with Kara and the President. In fact there wasn't much for Halder to be President of, but he'd been elected properly, and we intended to keep Mars democratic.

"But you admit yourself that this is nonsense," he said, scratching his nose nervously. "What if nothing happens?"

"Then I explain it away. I'm an astrologer. We always have an excuse. You're still sending constant messages to the ship, I take it?"

Halder looked at Kara, who nodded. "But never a reply," she said.

"So you'll have told them about Martian astrology?"

She looked embarrassed. "Only a little."

"Then tell them everything. And tell them about the triad. Earth, Phobos, and Eurydice. Tell them it means something."

Halder took his hand from his nose, only for it to land on his ear. "But what is this supposed to achieve?"

"It gives them a cue," I said. "It gives them a deadline. If they're alive, they're trying to solve whatever's gone wrong, but they've probably got used to it. This says, Mars expects something on this day. Take the risk, go the extra mile. If you're going to do something, do it now. And besides," I spoke to Kara again. "After all this time, have you really got anything new to tell them?"

Halder looked at Kara, who merely shrugged. "Very well," he said. "Teach them Martian astrology. Tell them we all believe it, and tell them that it all kicks off with the triad."

...

Eurydice in Scorpio

You are at your most resourceful, able to solve any problem that comes your way. Because you will need to.

...

Within a day, everyone on Mars knew about my prediction. So did Earth, and if they were listening, so did Eurydice.

Everyone on Mars is a celebrity; there are too few of us to be unknowns. But my own status increased dramatically with my nonsensical deadline. I was broadcast throughout the dome, and although the presenter shook her head comically afterwards, she told us to tune in on the day.

Halder came to me for another reading. He wanted to know about triad day.

"It will be in Capricorn," I said. "Your leadership will come to the fore." (It is meaningless and harmless to tell a President he has leadership skills.)

He nodded. He seemed less nervous than when I had last seen him, as if he had finally made a difficult decision.

"The triad is a deadline for me as well as for Eurydice," he said. "The dome won't last forever, and we don't have the tools to mine for new materials. We need what's on the ship. If they don't move, we will."

"Should you be telling me this?" I said.

"Nothing is secret here. We'll build tools with what we can, mine what we can, recycle what we can. And finally, we'll create what we need to bring the cargo to Mars."

I looked at him, not understanding.

"A missile," he said.

...

Eurydice in Sagittarius

The most important thing to you now is your freedom. But you are not free.

...

If I hadn't set the deadline for Jerrett's freedom, I'd set it for his execution. The Martian colonists would work together to build the device that knocked Eurydice out of its orbit, crashing it to the surface so we could salvage what we could. And bury its dead.

And I realised that I would help them build it. We did not come here to be trapped in a single dome, waiting for it to break down and expose us to the elements. We were here to make this world the second human planet. We were here to take over Mars as we had taken over Earth.

Fragments of my husband would rain over us as the price.

Finally, I realised the nature of the deadline I had set. It would be the day when I was free to move on. Jerrett either lived and was on his way, or was presumed dead.

Kara came to my room later that evening, not for a reading but just for company. She, too, knew of Halder's decision. We talked into the night, about trivia and fantasies, memories of the distant past, and dreams of the far future. We didn't mention Eurydice, and I didn't ask her the question I had never asked, who she knew on the ship. And she didn't tell me.

And above us the ship kept to its orbit, as if oblivious to deadlines.

...

Eurydice in Capricorn

Now is the time to take on responsibilities and leadership, even if the only person you can lead is yourself.

...

I was in the control room on the day itself. A camera was pointed at me, and I was being interviewed by the same presenter who had shaken her head when I first made my prediction. Kara was sending regular messages to Eurydice and listening out for any replies, while Halder sat grim faced. And it was Kara who first broke the news.

"It's moving," she said.

We all rushed to where she sat, as if there were a picture of the ship on a screen. In fact, none of us understood any of the numbers that scrolled up.

"The ship's moving?" I said, incredulous.

"It's broken orbit."

"But what about landing craft? Shuttles?"

"It's broken orbit," she repeated.

"But it can't land," I said.

Halder understood what was happening. "Where is it heading, Kara?" he asked.

"Impossible to tell," she said. "But it's going outwards. At a guess, back to Earth."

Halder nodded to himself, as if he'd been expecting this. "What's Earth saying?" I asked.

"Nothing," she said. "They've broken off all communication." She looked up at me then, a wonderful shot for the camera. "Nice one," she said to me.

...

Eurydice in Aquarius

Cling to your independence. Break all ties. Run from restrictions. You can regret it another time.

...

I struggled to think. "Mars is a one-way trip," I said. "They can't carry the fuel or supplies for a return journey. Not with the people and equipment as well."

"Nonetheless, they're leaving," said Halder. "Looks like they had the fuel after all."

"But then. . ." It didn't make any sense. "They always intended to go home. They were never going to land."

"Still no signal from Earth," said Kara. "They've left us."

Halder left the room.

"We needed that equipment."

"The hell we did," said Kara. I saw that she was shaking with rage, and it seemed to be directed at me. "We'll have difficulty making it on our own, but we'll manage it. We'll open mines. It will be slow, but we'll never give up. The more we achieve, the faster we'll go. And the day will come when we'll rebuild Orpheus and send it back to Earth. And when we arrive, they'd better have better answers than a—" She stood up and spat the last word into my face. "—a triad!"

I waited until everyone else had left, almost frightened by the sense of overriding purpose that had glared in Kara's eyes. I knew that the other colonists would agree, and that Halder would open the first clumsy mines as soon as was physically possible.

"So that's why they did it," I said out loud. Then I went to my room, and packed up all my charts. We wouldn't be needing them any more.

...

Eurydice in Pisces

And now to remember compassion, and remember that cycles don't begin or end, they just keep on cycling.

...

Actually, I've no idea where Eurydice is any more. My computer could tell me, but no one cares.

16

I was right about Halder. I've never seen him move so fast. Our tools are toys, and our skills are weak, but once we start mining for metals, we can make better tools. We can take over this planet without waiting for the next handout from the mother world. If I were still practising astrology, I would change the meanings: Earth would become the thing you most hate, and Eurydice would be your traitorous side, the part that works against you.

Kara waited only until the next day before coming to see me.

"I wanted to apologise," she said. "I shouldn't have been so rude to you yesterday. In fact, your deadline did us all a favour."

I shrugged. "Everyone blames Orpheus for looking back," I said. "No one ever considered that Eurydice didn't leave the Underworld because she didn't want to."

"I wouldn't know," she said. "I only know that Earth and Eurydice have given us a sense of purpose we've never had before."

I didn't tell her that I thought this was deliberate, and she gave me an awkward hug. It was awkward because it went on too long, and I thought, to hell with Jerrett, to hell with Earth, to hell with the stars, and to hell with the old myths. We'll make our own stories now.

About the Author

Neil James Hudson is a UK-based writer who has published more than 20 stories in zines such as *Nemonymous, On The Premises,* and *Ballista.* Third Flatiron welcomes Neil back for his second appearance.

*****~~~~~*****

Make Carrots, Not War

by Maureen Bowden

Rhea Silvia stirred, stretched her legs, and stubbed her toe on her sleeping lover's breastplate, which was lying, with the rest of his armour, scattered around the leafy grove. "Ow!" she yelled.

With a warrior's instinct, Mars leaped out of sleep and onto his feet. "Where is he? Where's my sword? Where am I?"

"It's okay, Mars," she said. "Your ironmongery attacked my toe. Come here and give me a cuddle."

He rubbed his eyes and glanced at the sundial. "I can't stay any longer, Silvie. I've been AWOL for three days. Jupiter will be hurling thunderbolts."

"I don't want you to go," she said.

"I don't want to go, either. It wasn't my idea to be god of war. I wanted to be a farmer."

"Couldn't Jupiter get your brother, wossname, to do it?"

"Quirinus, you mean? Nah, I suggested that, but he said I looked better in the armour." He adjusted his codpiece, and Silvie handed him his helmet. "That's the trouble with Jupe. It's all about image with him." He kissed her for the last time. "Will you go back to the Vestal Virgins?"

"I can't. I've lost my qualification."

"You needn't worry," he said. "I'll have a word with Venus. She renews her virginity every time she takes a bath. I'm sure she'll be able to sort yours out."

"You'd ask your wife to do that?"

"Oh, she's my wife in name only. That was Jupe's idea too. 'Perfect couple,' he said. The truth is she's got more boyfriends than there are snakes on a gorgon's bonce."

"Off you go then, and thanks for planting the carrots. I'll think of you when I eat them."

...

"Where the Hades have you been?" the thunder god thundered. "The Assyrians have been decapitating and disembowelling for days, and not a flicker from the god of war."

"Calm down, Jupe," Mars said. "You'll be instigating climate change. They haven't missed me. I've said all along humans can't wait to kick the shit out of each other. They don't need me to encourage them to do it."

"You're missing the point, Mars. When they realise they don't need gods, they'll become atheists, and where does that leave us? Snuffed out of existence, that's where."

"But I wanted to be a farmer. That would be more use to them."

"Tell you what. I'll give you agriculture as your second portfolio, but war comes first. Now, get out and do your job."

Before he left Olympus, Mars called on Venus in her boudoir. "Can I ask a favour, Ve?"

"I suppose you want me to put your girlfriend's hymen back together again, right?"

"Were you watching me and Silvie?"

"Of course I was, you dingbat. I'm the goddess of love. It's what I'm supposed to do." She sat up, kicked a satyr out of bed, and re-fluffed her pillows. "Unfortunately, it'll be nine months before I can do a reconstruction job. You planted more than carrots, big boy. She's expecting twins."

His head spun. He was going to be a dad. "Will she be okay?"

"She'll have to be, won't she? Don't worry. I'll take care of her. You get on with your godding. Or whatever it is you do."

...

He oversaw the rise and fall of Rome, and he stayed in Britannia after the legions left. He put in an appearance when the Vikings showed up, but the Valkyrie chased him. "Oi!" Hilda said. "You're in the wrong mythology. Sling your hook."

At Hastings he squirmed as Harold Godwinson jumped when he should have ducked, and got an eye full of arrow.

He went once more into the breach at Harfleur, and he joined the band of brothers at Agincourt, but Henry V didn't need any help.

The Wars of the Roses gave him a headache. He wasn't sure which side he was supposed to be on, but neither was anyone else. He did, however, let the princes out of the tower when nobody was looking. They ran off to Wales and took up sheep farming in Snowdonia. He envied them.

He was prepared to defend Good Queen Bess against the Spanish Armada, but Neptune had it covered. He found him wrecking King Philip's ships off the coast of France. "Still making waves, Nep?" he said.

The old seadog grinned, giving an obscene gesture with his trident. "If you don't use it man, you lose it."

In the English civil war he cheered on the Cavaliers, but they lost. He'd realised by then that he wasn't cut out for the career that had been foisted upon him, so he went to Ireland and planted potatoes in County Cork. He stayed until the potato famine drove him back to England in the middle of the nineteenth century, wishing he'd stuck to carrots.

He felt he should do his bit when the First World War broke out, so he conned his way into the Salvation Army, learned to play the trumpet, and served cups of tea to the lads in the trenches. He sang "Pack Up Your Troubles In Your Old Kit Bag" with Tommy Atkins, and he cradled Tommy's head in his arms as he died. He escorted his soul to the banks of the Styx, after taking a detour to Mount Olympus and helping himself to a handful of gold nuggets from Jupiter's stash.

Charon the ferryman was waiting for Tommy's soul. Mars helped him into the boat, gave the gold to the ferryman, and said, "Take him wherever he wants to go."

Charon saluted. "Yessir," he said.

When the war ended, he sold his armour to a scrap metal merchant and gave the proceeds to the British Legion. They gave him a poppy. After the end of the Second World War he carried an emaciated child out of Auschwitz, and he wept.

When the nuclear age dawned, politics became too complicated, and he gave up godding for good. In the 1960s he grew his hair long and sang, "Give Peace a Chance."

...

Whilst walking in the Moorland hills of Lancashire, in Northern England, he spotted a sign nailed on a farm gate, "Farmhand Wanted, Apply Within." It wasn't much of a farm—a couple of acres and a few chickens strutting around the yard, but to Mars it was the Elysian Fields.

He knocked at the door. An old man answered. Mars said, "I've come about the job."

"Come in, lad. I'm George. What's your name?"

"Mars. . . den," he corrected himself, "Kevin Marsden."

"Any relation to Gerry? You'll never walk alone, and all that?"

"I don't think so."

"Just my little joke, son. This is my wife, Alice."

The elderly lady said, "I'll put the kettle on."

22

Make Carrots, Not War

"We can't pay much," George said, "but you'll get bed and board and good food. The work's not hard, but me and Al are getting on a bit, and we can't quite manage it anymore."

"Don't you have family?" Mars said.

"Twin boys. They died in the war."

For the first time in over two thousand years, Mars thought of Silvie and his own twins. "I'm sorry," he said. "I'm a pacifist. I steer clear of wars."

"You do right, lad," Alice said, as she handed him a cup of tea and two digestive biscuits.

He took the job, he grew carrots, and he was content. After George died, Alice said, "You've been like a son to us, Kev. I'm leaving you the farm in my will."

"Don't talk like that, Ma," he said. "You've got years left in you yet."

"No, I'll not be long behind George." She was right. Six months later she was dead. He accompanied her to the Styx, after another detour to Olympus for the ferryman's fare. Jupiter's palace was deserted—not a god in sight. They'd been snuffed out. Mars had adapted to changing times; the other Olympians hadn't. He suspected Venus was still around, possibly running a brothel in Bangkok. She was a survivor. He grabbed the gold, and they left.

Charon's eyes lit up when he saw Mars. George was waiting with him. The old couple climbed into the boat together. The ferryman took Mars's gold, and Alice called to him as he waved goodbye, "Get yourself a nice girl, Kevin."

He returned to the farm, retrieved the "Farmhand Wanted" sign from behind the chicken coop, and nailed it onto the gate. A couple of days later, he was digging up carrots, when a once-familiar voice said, "Hello, Mars."

He turned. Rhea Silvia was wearing flared denims, a tight vest-top, and no bra. She was looking good. "Hello, Silvie," he said. "It's Kevin now."

23

"It suits you," she said.

"What are you doing here?"

"Applying for the job."

"You didn't go back to the Vestal Virgins, then?"

"Not much call for intact hymens these days."

"No, I suppose not. I heard about the twins. I'm sorry."

"Me too. It was a shame about Remus. Romulus made quite a name for himself, though."

"Did Venus take good care of you?"

"You could say that. She made me immortal. It's a mixed blessing."

"The trick is to keep busy."

"Still growing carrots, I see."

"Silvie, people will always need carrots."

"Do I get the job, then?"

"Grab a spade."

About the Author

Maureen Bowden is an ex-patriate Liverpudlian living with her musician husband on the island of Anglesey, off the coast of North Wales, where they try in vain to evade the onslaught of their children and grandchildren. She writes for fun and has had several poems and short stories published. She loves Rock 'n' Roll, Shakespeare, and cats. Third Flatiron is happy to welcome her back for a second apperance.

*****~~~~*****

Colorblind on the Red Planet

by Vince Liberato

"Jericho are you getting this? It's green. Green everywhere for miles." My hand over the visor of my suit, I stood on the surface of Mars for the first time.

"Wait, what? That's impossible. It's Mars. It has to be red."

"It's like an olive out here. Green as far as I can see. Switch to my suit's camera so you can get this." I smiled. Jericho had forgotten I was colorblind.

"I'm trying. I think your hand's in the way. Marcus, get it off the camera!" he said.

I moved my hand. Jericho swore in my headset, and I did not even try to stifle my laugh.

"You liar," he finally said, laughing a little.

"I can't be lying when I can't tell the difference between green and red."

"But you said it was olive green. You should know that olives are normally. . ." he started, then swore again. "Fine. You got me. The pits are red. . . Or so you've been told, right? What are the readings out there?"

I looked down at the spectrometer and read the numbers back to Jericho. We could have sent a machine out, but it was the first chance we had to go outside, and I had drawn the short straw. It was a clear day. Peaceful. A perfect day for a walk on the planet's surface. A shame the tool in my hands was telling me otherwise. Anchored against the side of the Tartarus Montes, we would be safe from the oncoming storm. It was unlikely that we would even notice it from inside, but after what happened to the First Martian Expedition, dust storms were treated as high tier threats. I flipped the spectrometer off and let myself back in the Fort. Trips outside would be scheduled on the planet's terms, not mine, leaving us, the Second Martian Expedition, safe inside the Fort during bad weather.

...

Jericho and the rest of the crew were waiting for me when I got out of sterilization. I had changed into the skintight jumpsuits made out of the spandex/rubber/silk hybrid material engineered for the mission and left the space suit by the main room's terminal. There were four of us—Jericho, myself, Lily, and Katja. Our habitat, nicknamed the Fort, was a ship built to anchor and drill itself directly into the side of a mountain. Only a massive circular door exposed itself to the outside world, while the rest was tucked away inside thick rock that worked in tandem with the titanium skin of the Fort to keep us safe from the elements. It was a self-sustained environment that would never be moved again, designed from the ground up after the failure of the first expedition. If we were successful, there would be several others in that mode and model to come. There was already talk of hollowing out Olympus Mons and creating the equivalent to a human ant hill, a shelter like the Fort large enough to house thousands or even millions. Several large corporations were already bidding and submitting designs, dissecting the planet's mountain ranges and staking claims for widespread colonization of the red planet.

All they were waiting on was for us to survive a full Earth year. Prove that it could be done after what had happened the first time Man was on Mars.

"What's up?" I asked the group.

Katja spoke. "Farming floor's up and running. We'll be growing our own food in a few weeks. Maybe sooner."

Jericho followed. "Water supply's fully stocked. Even if our collectors in the uniforms and air con didn't recycle every drop of everything wet that comes out of us, we have enough water to last us a decade, maybe longer."

"Air?" I asked, already knowing the answer.

26

"Breathable. And abundant." Lily adjusted her uniform before speaking. I knew she was not happy about how it clung to her, but it was all she had to wear.

"How abundant?"

"You'll die of thirst before you suffocate."

"Enough," Jericho said. "We want to know how outside felt. How was the suit?"

"Like a second skin. I could feel the surface of the planet under my toes. It's almost as great as our regular uniform." I shot a look at Lily, who glared back.

Katja spoke next. "Those readings were pretty strong. You sure you didn't feel anything?"

"No. I swear I could feel the dust between my toes, even a slight breeze, but nothing like the storm the data suggests."

"Hold that thought. Wow. . . It's just. . . you need to look at this." Lily motioned for us to get to the monitor she was watching. Sure enough, it was the twister out of the *Wizard of Oz* come to life. Double for me because of my color blindness, only there would be no Technicolor Munchkinland afterwards.

"Guess we're not going anywhere," Jericho said. He was right.

We made small talk for a few minutes before heading to the dining room for dinner. All of us were in our late twenties, selected a decade ago and trained for our mission. The First Martian Expedition was comprised of scientists, athletes, doctors—the best mankind had to offer. And not a week after their ship touched down, one of them opened a door during a dust storm, killing everyone. It was reported as an accident, but anyone who understood ship design would know better. Locks had to be overridden, artificial intelligence shut off, and then the doors manually opened. By the time a probe was able to investigate, the Martian atmosphere had done its job, completely wiping out all records of what had occurred. It was decided that the next expedition would be as different as possible and the habitat redesigned to babysit its inhabitants until it was sure that they would not kill themselves, thus us and the Fort. The Thousands of teenagers were scouted and recruited and trained for a decade not only for the necessary jobs around the Fort, but also to retain the qualities that made young adults different from traditional space explorers. By the time we four were selected, we were at the peak of physical conditioning and fully capable of running, repairing, and researching the Fort and Mars. But most importantly, we liked each other, had worked well together for years, and did not bring the baggage that the crew of the First Mars Expedition had. Whoever thought that putting the most accomplished people in the world together and expecting them to follow orders did not know anything about the effects of ego and celebrity, and how that would affect a chain of command where people had to be told what to do.

...

Night in the Fort was dictated by the lighting system that adjusted itself to its occupants. Hall lights lit up as we approached and turned off when we passed during the night hours and remained permanently on during the day. Several of the walls were adorned with "windows," screens that would display images based on the preference of the crew member nearing them that remained off otherwise. Katja had the beach, Jericho had a snowy mountain, Lily a lakeside forest, and I, the hill country during the fall. Yellow was one of the only colors I was able to discern due to my handicap. The golden grass bending slightly, as if in the wind, could always cheer me up.

I walked the long halls, running my fingers on every window I passed. The rest of the crew had retired for the night, Jericho and Katja in her room and Lily in mine. She had curled up and was asleep by the time I had dressed. For the next six months, outside of the occasional walk on the surface, we were not allowed to do much of anything outside of take atmospheric readings and entertain ourselves with the plethora of distractions and entertainments given to us by our bosses. We would not be given access to the Fort's higher systems until we passed a sanity test to be given to us six months after touching down on the Martian soil. Even our walks on the surface were limited by the single suit we would have to share. In the uppermost level of the Fort, we knew there were hundreds more, as well as a master control station we were not allowed to touch yet. The combination to the lock on its door would be given after all functioning crew members were declared sane and any that were not locked away in quarantine.

Ahead, one of the windows was somehow on; its faint radiance was almost unnoticeable in the darkness. I took a few more steps. The ceiling light flickered to life, and the window's glow remained. Closing the gap, I stood parallel to the window. At the proper angle I should have been able at to view the endless, comforting fields. They were there, but the picture was blurred. I reached up to the top of the window and flipped a switch. The meadows went away, and in its place was an orb colored in a hue I had never seen before. It was similar to yellow, but also like black with a faint blue glow. It looked like it was placed right behind the glass in the window. I turned it back on and then off a few more times, finally leaving the window off and heading down the hall to Katja's room. I had to show everyone.

Outside, the storm raged on.

...

"There are some reports," Jericho said, "that say that people with red/green color-blindness can see other colors that we can't. That. . . That could be a possibility. Maybe there is something there. Maybe he sees something we can't."

"There's nothing out there. We can't let him out."
Katja was pacing back and forth. "Not after what he did to
Lily."

After Jericho and Katja had seen nothing wrong
with the window, we went to get Lily to see if she could
see what I did. As we walked the hallways, the
temperature dropped significantly, something the
safeguards in the Fort were supposed to prevent. We all
noticed it, but did not have much time to reflect, because
we were at my room. The door opened, and we saw Lily
in a pool of her own blood.

A trenchlike cut etched her throat, limbs, and
trunk, like a river marked on a map. The blood glowed
faintly with the same neon that was on the door and
window. Before I could say anything, the first punch
caught me in the solar plexus, the second came down on
my back, and a kick to my temple knocked me out. I
awoke in quarantine, listening to Katja and Jericho. It was
cold. Very cold.

"Don't you feel that?" I pounded on the glass. "It's
freezing!"

They ignored me and continued to argue. My
breath started to fog the glass on my cell, and I wiped it
away. It was faint, but on the floor close to where Jericho
was standing, I could see the strange color, concentrated
this time, in a blob about the size of my fist. I yelled a
warning and Jericho turned, unaware of the orb and
bringing his foot down on top of it.

The effect was instant. He collapsed, flailing his
arms and legs as he fell. The same gashes that were on
Lily ripped into his body, pulling skin and muscle apart,
tracing major veins and arteries down to the bone.
Seconds later, he was still. Dead. The entire time, he did
not make a sound.

"Katja, let me out!" I yelled. "I saw what he
stepped on. I can see it. I can. . ." Along the floor and
ceiling, more of the spheres appeared, oozing out like pus

from a wound. "Katja, freeze. Do not bring your foot down."

She obeyed.

"Do you see them?" I shouted.

"See what?" She was looking around the room. "What are you talking about? What's going on?"

"Katja, you're going to have to listen to me. Make one wrong move, and you'll end up like Jericho and Lily." I told her to step backwards and instead to walk a strange path to the door I was locked behind. She undid the lock and let me out.

"Listen," I told her. "There are little balls all over the ground that I can see. It's that color I was telling you about. What happened to Jericho, he stepped on one. I saw it. They're everywhere in this room. You need to follow me. Step exactly where I step."

"Marcus," she said. "I'm cold."

I told her I was too and then led her out of quarantine.

...

They were everywhere. Spread out in every room, on every wall, some in clusters and others solitary spots. If there was a pattern, I could not see it. Katja followed me, terrified, but careful to trace my every step. I was nervous, but I could see them. Without me, Katja had no way to perceive, much less avoid, the things. I was the only thing keeping her alive, although at the rate the temperature was falling I was not sure how much longer that was going to be. Our uniforms helped a little, but were not enough, especially if the temperature did not stabilize. We had to find a way to warm up the Fort, and we had to do it fast. Katja and I could worry about finding a solution to the infestation afterwards, but first, we had to get to the central room and the main computer to see why the Fort's heating was malfunctioning.

"What about the space suit?" she asked me as the door to the main room slid open.

"What about it?"

"That would keep one of us warm, wouldn't it?"

I thought for a moment. She was right, but there was only one, we both knew that. "I suppose it would," I answered. I waited to see if she was going to add anything else. When she did not, I changed the subject. "This room is really bad with those things. Do you want to stay here or keep following me?"

"I'll follow you."

"Okay, left foot first. Ready? Go."

To get to the computer, we had to run an invisible maze. This room was the biggest in the Fort, and the little orbs covered it. When possible, I kept my feet planted on the ground and snaked them forward, sliding with each step for Katja to mimic.

"You said they're like little balls?" Katja asked.

"Yeah. Just sitting here like landmines. Pretty sure this is what happened to the Firsties. Only because they couldn't see anything, they tried to clean out the place by opening the doors— probably guessed what was killing them."

"Makes sense," Katja said. "They crop up during dust storms and surround things alien to Mars. Like planetary antibodies. Still doesn't explain the cold."

"Maybe this will." I had just reached the computer. A few feet away, the space suit was hanging up, thankfully free of the spheres. I looked at the readings and said nothing.

"What is it?"

"Fort's vitals are all reading clear. Somehow, every thermometer thinks it's really hot right now." I looked up, where I knew the main room's temperature reading equipment was positioned. There was a knot of the killer spheres on it. "They're messing with its readings. The thermometers all read 120, so the cold is from the Fort is trying to counteract it."

"Can't you do anything?" Katja asked.

"No. Maybe if it were one thermometer acting up, but I can't convince the Fort that they're all incorrect. It'll think I'm trying to kill everyone."

"What about calling back home? Ask Earth for help."

"Can't. All our comm equipment is covered too. We're stuck. Only thing we can do is wait for the upstairs room to unlock." We looked at each other, and both of us turned to the space suit.

"Please," she whimpered when her eyes met mine. "Don't. . ."

I pushed her. "I'm sorry," I said as she stepped back onto one of the orbs and died in front of me. I took the suit and put it on and was able to find some comfort in the warmth that followed. Six months, I just needed to last that long. There was no other choice.

I had no other choice.

...

Greetings crew of Second Martian Expedition. Six months ago today you landed on Mars. Congratulations! For the sake of formality, we only ask that you answer the following questions as a measure of your mental health. All answers will be given orally, so we ask that you answer in as slow and calm a manner as possible. So please, sit down, relax and answer the following questions.

Question one: How are you feeling today?

"Send help. Please send help. Get me out of here. I can't move from this room. There's nothing. Nothing except me and these Martian baseballs. That's what I call them. They kill you if you touch them. Nobody can see them but me. Please. Get help. Get me out of here. Please. I'm begging you. Every storm that goes through leaves more of them here. Don't send anyone else to Mars. Just get me out of here.

Please?

Can you hear me? Is anyone there?"

Redshifted: Martian Stories

The computer sent out a signal to Earth to indicate that the Second Martian Expedition failed and that the Fort would need to be abandoned until salvage operations could be finalized. Operations for the Third Martian Expedition began the next day.

###

About the Author

Vince Liberato is the author of a handful of short stories, most recently "The Remnants of Civilization" published in Almond Press's After the Fall apocalyptic anthology and "World Collide and Then Separate" featured in Demonic Visions: 50 Horror Tales. He enjoys plotting out futures that he would prefer not to live in and explaining this flavor of insanity to his reluctant girlfriend/editor. At the moment, he lives in Texas.

*****~~~~~*****

The Journal of Miss Emily Carlton

by Lela E. Buis

July 12, 1915

When John Carter's nephew published the accounts of his adventures in 1911, it ignited many an imagination. It was barely three years later that Professor Bannister approached my father with the idea of mounting an expedition to the planet Mars.

He first sent a letter of introduction requesting an appointment, but of this I knew nothing. My first awareness of his existence was when he arrived at our townhouse in Boston with his son Edward. The two men were early for the appointment, and Laurence, our butler, answered the door bell. My father and I were on the terrace watching my younger brothers play croquet, and their happy voices rose in laughter when Elmer made an especially good shot. I was glad to have some time with my father, but this was interrupted when Laurence appeared at the French doors.

"Mr. Carlton," he said. "A Professor Bannister to see you?"

"Ah, yes," said my father. He stuck his cigar between his teeth and reached into his waistcoat for his pocket watch. "The man is early," he noted. "He must be damned eager. Ah, well," he went on. "Emily, if you will excuse me?"

He took hold of my wheelchair and pushed it through the French doors.

"Laurence," he said. "Tell Lizette I have an appointment. She will need to take Miss Carlton upstairs."

"Yes, sir," said Laurence.

The two departed in different directions, my father to his study down the hall and Laurence, presumably, to

35

locate Lizette. I arranged the ruffles and folds of my white dress and resigned myself to wait. Meanwhile, I heard the murmur of voices down the hallway, and then a conversation taking place in the study. My father had failed to close the door.

Someone, presumably Professor Bannister, said, "Thank you for allowing me to present my plans. Any funding you could provide would be greatly welcome."

"Well," said my father. "You do think you have a workable plan?"

"Of course," said Professor Bannister, rattling papers. "The red planet isn't that far away. It would be hardly more difficult to plot a course than it was for Mr. Barbicane to carry out an expedition to the moon in 1865. His equipment is still in place near Tampa, and it could be repaired and modified."

I didn't understand what they were talking about, but I was already weary of waiting for Lizette. The townhouse had a parlor across from the entry and stairs, and my father's study was just behind that. The hallway wrapped from the entry around it, leading past the kitchen and scullery to the French doors that gave onto the garden—where my chair was just then located. However, the lift was in the front of the house, and in order to get to my room upstairs, I would have to negotiate the hallway. My wheelchair was fairly compact, but it was still difficult to make the turns.

It was possible that Lizette was gone on an errand, so I resolved to make my way to the lift alone. Because I am afflicted, I had difficulty in grasping the wheels of the chair with any command, but I managed to make the turn at the corner of my father's study quite well. However, I encountered difficulty in getting through the doorway into the entry. The wheelchair caught on the doorframe, and I tried to back up. However, it seemed stuck fast, and I struggled with it, privately cursing the weakness in my arms. I was suddenly near tears.

"Excuse me," said a voice. "May I help you?"

The voice was strange, flat and tinny like a gramophone recording. When I looked around, I saw the most amazing thing. It appeared to be a clockwork man.

He was standing in the doorway of the parlor. His face and hands were the pale silvery color of aluminum, and he was well dressed in a suit with a waistcoat and trousers.

I gaped at him. "My God," I finally managed to say. "Who are you?"

"I'm Edward Bannister," he said. "Are you Mr. Carlton's daughter?"

"I. . . yes," I said, aware that we were alone. "I'm Emily Carlton."

"Well, Miss Carlton," he said. "Could you use a hand with the chair?"

I was totally fascinated. "Never mind," I said. "Could you take me into the parlor, please?"

He took hold of the chair and turned it around so that we went into the parlor instead of toward the lift.

"Here?" he asked, indicating a place in the center of the Turkish carpet. "Will this be suitable?"

"It's fine," I said.

The parlor was papered in large roses, and the furniture was dark mahogany. Mr. Bannister had been sitting on a Toscano gossip bench with rose-flowered upholstery. He sat back down, apparently a trifle uneasy with my presence.

It would be rude to ask what he was, I thought, so I resolved to ask about the professor instead.

"Are you Professor Bannister's. . .?" I started.

". . . son," he finished for me.

"And your father has an appointment with mine?" I asked.

"Yes," he said. "About financing."

"Financing for what?" I asked.

So then he told me about the romantic accounts of John Carter regarding his adventures on Mars, and also about Jules Verne's account of Mr. Barbicane's trip to the moon and how these had inspired his father.

"And are you planning to be part of the expedition, Mr. Bannister?"

"My father means for me to pilot the craft," he said.

I hesitated. "Is that why you. . .?"

I had been wondering if, like Geppetto, his father had been moved to create a mannequin for a son. I was uncertain how to finish the question, but he took my meaning.

"I have my own brain," he said. "I was dying of consumption, and my father built this body for me to use when my own failed. I have volunteered to fly the spacecraft."

The loss of his body seemed a sad thing to admit, but I could see no evidence of emotion in him except for a slight flutter of his aluminum hands. Did dreams and emotions require a body to work?

"I am so sorry for your loss," I said.

"And what is your malady, Miss Carlton?" he asked then. It seemed decidedly forward, but I had pried into his personal circumstances only the moment before.

"I suffer from cerebral palsy," I said, trying to lift my chin bravely.

There seemed to be no pity in him as I normally saw in the faces of people I met—especially in men. However, he responded in immediate sympathy. He lifted one of his light, finely jointed hands and laid it on mine where I clutched the arm of the wheelchair.

At that moment, I heard my father and Professor Bannister coming down the hallway. I quickly removed my hand from Edward's grasp.

"Have you a card?" I asked, and was pleased when he took one from his vest pocket and laid it in my palm without a word. I closed my fingers over it tightly.

"Thank you, sir," Professor Bannister was saying. "I will most certainly send more diagrams and calculations for your edification.

"Edward. . ." he said then, letting his son know that he was ready to leave.

My father and the professor stopped in the hallway to shake hands, and when Edward rose, my father looked through the doorway and saw me sitting there.

"Why, Emily," he said. "I thought you had gone upstairs."

"I had started, father," I said. "Lizette did not come, and Mr. Bannister rescued me when I got stuck in the hallway."

"Er, why thank you, sir," said my father.

"It was my pleasure to help," said Edward. "Mr. Carlton, you have a lovely daughter."

I thought he was talking about my dress, as he certainly couldn't have meant me.

After they were gone, I asked, "Father, what did you think of the clockwork man?"

"An amazing accomplishment," he said. "It gave me confidence in Professor Bannister, and I will be providing financial backing for him."

I was glad to hear that, as it meant that I might see them again. Over the fall and winter, Edward and I kept up a weekly correspondence. Because of my infirmity, I had perforce become something of a woman of letters, and I found in Edward a like mind. The Bannisters moved from New York to Tampa in the early fall so the professor could see to modifications of Barbicane's space cannon. During the long, dark winter, I sat by the fire and tried to visualize Edward on the red plains of the distant world. After Christmas, I became confident enough of his regard to send him some of my poetry. Written and hidden away in secret, it expressed my own yearnings and my deepest feelings about life, death, and the condition of my soul. He never failed to be supportive.

I had the thought that perhaps his metal body was something like my wheelchair, only a conveyance. Still it was infinitely worse to be in his condition. He wrote to me of watching the sea and hearing the waves and the gulls, but not being able to feel the waves washing around his ankles. Although aluminum does not rust, still it corrodes, and he could not swim in the surf as he had as a human man. The metal body was heavy, and he hoped the smaller gravity of Mars would lighten it.

That struck me as phenomenal, as I had not considered gravity. Would it work for me as well, I wondered? Could I walk there as others did?

By early fall, Edward wrote that the capsule to be launched by the space cannon was done. He sent sketches so that I could see and understand the craft. The trip to Mars would take about 250 days, and the professor had prepared a potion for his son to drink that would leave him in a suspended state to conserve provisions. Soon the launch date was set, and my father meant to attend. I begged to go along.

"Emily," he said, "the trip will be too difficult for your delicate constitution."

"Lizette can come along," I argued. "I want to see the ocean, father."

"Ah, if your mother were here. . . " he said.

She had died of typhoid about five years before, and he knew how much she would have enjoyed the trip. The thought seemed to convince him that my request was reasonable, and he gave his permission.

I was hugely excited, as I had never been on a trip before. Lizette packed a large trunk, and we took a car to South Station. The interior was like a cathedral, with high, arched windows and light that streamed in like molten gold. Sounds echoed off the masonry walls. Lizette was as excited as I was. She stayed close by, as if afraid she would be left behind if she strayed too far. My father was totally relaxed. He sat in one of the chairs in the waiting area and read the evening papers.

The train itself was terrifying. The engine was huge and black, and it spat dark smoke. We found our car and our Pullman suite. The seats made into beds, and Lizette took the upper bunk and I the lower one. We slept like babies to the clattering of the wheels. In the morning, we were passing through cotton fields in Georgia, but it still took most of the day to reach Tampa.

The Bannisters were both at Union Station to meet us. I felt shy at seeing Edward again, as my mental image of him had changed through the course of his letters. It would take a few hours to reconcile his appearance with the tender flow of his correspondence.

We took lodging at the Tampa Bay Hotel, and Professor Bannister and Edward had dinner with us that evening in the hotel dining room. My father and the professor were deeply engaged in conversation about the impending spaceflight. I ordered red snapper, which turned out to be delicious.

"Father," I said, finally. "Could I go to the beach tomorrow?"

"I'm going to tour the facility and see the controls for the space cannon," he said.

"But. . ." I began, and Edward interrupted.

"Mr. Carlton," he said. "I'd be happy to take Emily to the beach."

My father hesitated, and I said, "Lizette can come along."

"That is why you came, isn't it, dear?" he asked.

"Of course," I said

I was sure he meant the beach, but I was happy that I would have some time with Edward.

The morning dawned clear and bright. The wheelchair ran well enough on the boardwalk, but not in the sand. Lizette put up an umbrella, and Edward lifted me carefully in his metal arms and carried me down to where I could watch the waves. Lizette volunteered to go to a hot dog vendor to get lunch for us. There was only the sound of the surf as a backdrop for a conversation.

"Are you ready for the flight?" I asked.

"Yes, of course," he said. "There's not much to it, as the calculations for the orbital transfers are already done. The charge in the gun will launch the capsule, and I have only to make slight corrections in the speed at the end of the trip to have the planet capture the craft."

"Would that I could go with you," I said.

He made no answer. I dipped my hand onto the sand, where the broken bits of shell were all that was left of some departed bivalve, and let the fragments pour through my fingers.

"Edward, I'm serious," I said. "Do you think I could actually walk there?"

A couple strolled by and stared at us rudely, the pathetic, crippled girl in her swim suit and the metallic man who would corrode if he accidently fell into the sea.

"It's a crazy idea," he said finally.

"I'm a romantic," I said. "I want to be wild and free."

"Are you suicidal?" he asked.

"Aren't you?"

He shouldn't have been surprised. Some of my poetry was very dark, expressing a dreadful hopelessness and a fury at my inability to live in any way except within the confines of my chair. On better days, I was better reconciled, but still I often thought of death.

He was as insane as I was.

"You could go," he said finally. "I could give you the potion to drink, instead of drinking it myself. It slows the body so you wouldn't need much in the way of food and drink. A minor change in the calculations would take care of the extra weight."

The Journal of Miss Emily Carlton

My heart leaped that I had talked him into it. "You have only to find a way to hide me there until the moment."

"Tell Lizette you're ill," he said. "Drink the potion the night before, and I'll place you in the capsule. Everyone will think you safe in the hotel until it's too late."

I did as he suggested, and never felt the launch. Supposedly the G forces caused by the swift acceleration were near deadly, but I woke in the craft most of a year later, feeling in good health as we attained an orbit. I was extremely weak from the inactivity, but weakness was a normal state for me. Edward helped me to sit up, and I watched as he operated the controls to bring us down on the surface of the planet.

This was actually my first look at the capsule. It was about nine feet in diameter, much of it filled with equipment and stores. It was nearly dark, except for the lights from the instrument panels. I had brought only a small satchel for luggage and my journal.

"What happened as I slept?" I asked him.

"Not much," he said. "When I was close to the earth, I could talk to my father by radio, but eventually I lost contact."

"What did my father say about my disappearance?" I asked.

"He was greatly concerned," he said. "I believe the consensus was that you had gone to your death in the sea."

I had to laugh. "That was the right idea," I said, "but I have higher ambitions."

He turned his face to me, and I thought he would have smiled.

"Can we breathe the air?" I asked.

"Who knows?" he said.

"So we might die as soon as we open the hatch?"

"If not, then maybe we can explore," he said. "Wouldn't that be thrilling?"

43

He operated the controls with a sure hand, and the capsule deployed a parachute and crashed down with only a bone-jarring impact.

"If we don't immediately asphyxiate, we might live for a while," he said. The capsule has equipment to produce water and nutrients."

We waited for the capsule to cool, and for him to run tests on the air.

"It seems to be thin but breathable," he finally said.

He opened the hatch and climbed out, and after he had a look around he came back for me. I had already felt the difference in the gravity, and managed to pull up to a standing position. When he appeared above me, I held up my hand, and he lifted me through the hatch opening and set me on my feet. A red plain stretched in all directions, and in the distance a line of mountains silhouetted against the horizon. It was strangely beautiful.

"Where are the Martians?" I asked.

"Perhaps there are none," he said.

"Then what did John Carter write of?"

"An alternate universe?" he said. "A dream?"

To the east shone the bright disk of the morning star, and another blue jewel set against the vast magnitude of space. I reached out and took Edward's hand.

"Let's go," I said, and took my first step.

About the Author

Lela Buis' prose and poetry have been published by *Galaxy Magazine, Pirate Writings, Thirteenth Moon,* and various other magazines and anthologies. Some years ago, she was recognized as a quarter-finalist in the L. Ron Hubbard Writers of the Future Contest. She currently lives in Knoxville and is a member of the Knoxville Writers' Guild, the SFWA, and the Science Fiction Poetry

Association. That Ridge Press has recently released four collections of her short stories and poetry, and she is currently working on novel-length works. Watch for these in the future!

*****~~~~~*****

Redshifted: Martian Stories

The Canary and the Roach

by Ian Rose

As I stare out the elevator glass over the rusty hills outside, I know one thing for certain: This place is not for me. With everything that's happened, the whirlwind of hopeless hungry fear that has drawn me up and spun me around in the last few days, I find myself envying the roaches. They could walk out there if we let them. They could feel the red sand between their claws as I never will on my bare feet.

When the door opens, the glowing white of the hallway makes my eyes hurt. In the mines, it's black on black, shades of it that even in the direct light of a torch would be flattered to be called gray. Here in the tower, they've made a place immune to shadow, where they can forget the hard dark labor that sustains their luxury.

At the end of the hall, there's only one door, and I realize this whole floor is his office. No nameplate. It would break the aesthetic, I guess, the illusion of walking through a tunnel of pure light to a destination that could only be the right one. In the absence of choice, labels lose their necessity.

I step through, and the receptionist almost jumps out of his chair to greet me. The young man is tall and lean, his pale forehead topped with a little forest of blonde hair. I let myself think for a second that it looks a little like my hair when I take my helmet off after a long shift, but it's nothing like that. His sticks out and up because it's been cut and styled specifically to do so; mine does it because it's been drenched in sweat, sometimes spiced with blood.

"You must be Mr. Eckert. Can I take your. . ." He trails off when he realizes I'm not carrying a coat. Why anyone ever would, when every room in the colony is

47

maintained at the same temperature, I can't imagine. Probably the same reason a rich kid with a safe little office job pays to make his hair look like a canary's.

"He'll see you now." The receptionist leads me through another door to a tall chamber shaped like the inside of a soup can. Behind a semicircular fake-wood desk sits a chubby man in a gaudy green chair. Past him, a window overlooks the northern half of the colony and the ruddy expanse beyond. At the far northern end, I can see the oversized dome of the Governor's office. Just as we can look up from our crowded observation deck and see the executive tower rising above us, the company men's windows all face their master's house.

"Eckert," he says, standing and gesturing me to a chair opposite his. "Can I call you Jed?" I tell him he can.

"Fantastic. Call me Rome. I hope you found the place all right." He smiles like a mannequin, his face looking more like a design choice than an expression.

"Thank you for the invitation, Mr. Rome." I fold my hands on my lap. Even though I work in an airtight suit, and even having washed twice since crawling out of the mine, I still feel like I would leave a mark if I touched anything in this office.

"It's just Rome, actually. I started using it a few weeks ago. Everyone's been choosing single names for themselves lately, and I thought it sounded. . . regal. I resisted the trend for a while, but what can you do? We're all slaves to fashion." He pauses, but I have nothing at all to answer to that.

"Are you feeling all right? I hope we gave you enough time to rest up before we called you in."

"I'm fine, sir. Got a good night's sleep last night, and well into this morning. I was grateful for the days off."

He lost the plastic smile and nodded with an expression of forced sincerity. "Least we could do. That was a hell of a thing you did yesterday. I'd like to hear how it happened." He adds: "When did you first know something was wrong?"

The short answer, I tell him, is that I didn't know until it was already over. The canary who taught me the ropes when I first arrived on Mars told me that if there was ever a cave-in, that's how it would be. There's no ticking clock, no race to get everyone out before the collapse. True to our name, canaries are there to sniff out problems before they happen, but if something does go wrong, you barely have time to cover your head.

That's just what I did when I saw the first signs of the north tunnel coming down. I crouched down and covered my helmet with both arms. I closed my eyes, and thought of the memories I wanted with me in that moment. Lily on her grandma's porch, still young, sipping lemonade. Dad in his garden. My old dog Sam jumping on me like he always did when I got back from a long day at work. I've considered more than once what I'd choose as my last thoughts in this life, and those three images always win out.

When the rocks stopped falling, I realized I wasn't dead or even injured. The room had collapsed around me, but if anything landed on me, it wasn't heavy enough to feel through my pressure suit. The row lights were out, and so I was in pure darkness for the few seconds it took me to grab my emergency torch. In those long seconds, I was an astronaut. There are no directions in space, no meaningful dimensions when surrounded by infinite black. A mine's the same way, when the lights are out. I got my torch lit, and took note of where the walls had come down. All around me, roaches were still crawling back and forth, some with their sacs half full of ore, some empty. I saw their flat black shells scuttling around me, and wondered if they even recognized that anything had changed.

A roach isn't a complicated creature. Despite their nickname, they are only distantly related to the old Earth bug. We've gone far out of our way to make sure those particular nasties don't follow us out into the solar system. These roaches are derived from an African beetle, or that's what I've heard. Some company whiz kids a few decades back got the task of creating a new species to help us mine, one that wouldn't need much food or water and could survive on Martian atmosphere without a suit. What they gave us is a beetle about the size of a large dog, but flatter to the ground, with a reinforced carapace and a flexible dorsal sac that can carry up to a few hundred kilos of mineral back and forth.

I took my torch and inspected the corners of what was left of our tunnel. The cave-in had blocked off both ends, and I realized in a panic that I had no idea which of them was the southern side, the one that would lead back to base and a comforting bath of artificial light. That worry passed as I watched the roaches. They always mined away from the base until their ore sacs were full, oriented not by light but by some blind, innate sense of direction. The bugs trapped here with me were all clustering on one side. The other way would lead me home.

I should say, most of them were on the far end of the tunnel, not all. One sat still right next to me. When I first saw it, I thought it was dead, but its feet were moving just slightly, tapping against the floor as they tend to do when they aren't digging. I pointed my torch down and lit up its face. Antennae wiggled back and forth, and two big reflective black eyes stared straight up into mine. There was a red spot above its left eye, a rare distinguishing mark for a species engineered to be identical. I had gotten pretty lucky, when it came down to it.

I took note of the red mark and the lack of a dorsal sac, and confirmed that this was a messenger. A few roaches on each site are programmed to report to the canary for orders to pass on to the others. Statistically speaking, I wouldn't have expected one of the two dozen

50

trapped with me to be a messenger bug. I remember smiling down into its empty but somehow expectant eyes.

I reached down into my belt pack and got out the chem markers. Each canary goes into the mine with a set of three color-coded chemical markers for directing roaches. Each one gives a different chemical cue; there's green for dig, yellow for avoid, and blue for calm. You can use them on roaches directly, but it's far more efficient to mark paths and orders for the messenger and let it pass them on to the rest. I took out the blue marker and touched it to the messenger bug's face. It scrabbled past me and over to the others, who abruptly stopped their digging at the far wall. They all waited for my next order.

I walked over to the south end of the chamber and started laying down yellow on what looked like the most sensitive spots. The roaches will stay away from anything within a few centimeters of a yellow mark. Then I determined what I thought would be the best place to dig out a new tunnel, and marked that green. Once it was set up to my liking—something I admit to rushing a little, given that I had about an hour of air left in my tank—I found the messenger roach again and touched its face with my green marker. It passed the cue on to the others, and inside a minute they were all digging away where I had marked.

I sat and watched them work, and tried my best to control my breathing to make the most of the oxygen I had left. Likewise, the messenger had little to do once its cues were relayed, and it crawled back to sit next to me. Those saucer eyes peered up at me again, waiting for any additional commands.

Now here's the bit I don't tell the company man.

As I sat there, one eye on the roaches clawing away at the spots on the wall I had marked as safe, the other on my rapidly dwindling supply of air, I reached one hand down and started to stroke the carapace of that messenger roach. I'll always remember how it felt: hard

51

but reactive to touch. Even if I couldn't see what I was touching with those thick gloved fingers, I would have known it was alive.

With all the frantic digging going on only a few meters away, through the thin atmosphere and the solid glass of my helmet, I'm honestly not sure how I heard it. The messenger ground its teeth as I stroked its carapace, producing a subtle song of chitinous friction that I couldn't help but interpret as a purr. I thought of my old retriever back home, and from that point on, I called the messenger Sam.

The time on my oxy gauge had ticked down to ten minutes, and I woke myself up from these comforting distractions. I stepped over to the hole that the roaches had dug. It was impressive progress for fifty minutes of work, but the wall ahead of them was solid, and I had no way of knowing how much further they would need to go to hit the open air of the tunnel home. Panic took hold of me again. All I could think to do was to start pressing the red pen hard against the wall, stabbing it in an attempt to show the roaches how desperately I needed them to dig harder and faster. Red ink, and the behavioral cues it conveyed, dripped down over the stone and onto the backs of the roaches below.

I half-remembered something in my canary training about frenzies, when the roaches get overstimulated with cues and go wild. Whatever they told me about it, it didn't much matter to me then. I was eight minutes from suffocation, ten at most, and I had just wasted more in my scramble to mark the wall. I panted hard in my suit as the roaches began to frenzy.

What had been an orderly assembly line, with some bugs breaking up the rock and others carrying it back away from the new tunnel, exploded into chaos. Whether I had heard or imagined Sam's purring noise, I had no doubt of the sounds the other roaches were making now. Screeches, squeals, and a harder chorus of teeth

52

against shell filled up the dark. I wanted to point the light away, but I held it steady as I watched them chew and claw at not only the wall, but each other as well.

The needle on my oxy gauge was buried in red, flashing and warning me as if reminding me of something I had only forgotten. I was still sitting there, rubbing my hand over the long ridges in Sam's back and watching the carnage, when the lead digger opened a hole. They all clawed at it, pushing rocks both backward and ahead into the main tunnel, and in less than two minutes, they had made a space large enough for me to crawl through. I sprayed the calming blue marker all over the pile of roaches—and severed parts thereof—and proceeded to crawl over them, then ran with the last of my breath to the airlock. There was no one waiting there, no rescue team suiting up. One of the techs told me later that I had minutes, maybe seconds, before I would have started to experience the more brutal effects of hypoxia.

"Well, that's a hell of a story," Rome says as he stares over the desk at me. "Good thinking, inducing a frenzy. We try to avoid them at all costs, because of the damage they can cause, but in this case, it was the right call. We lost a fair number of roaches, but we got you back, and that's what matters to the company."

I thank him for that. He starts rattling off something about liability, and passes me some forms to sign. He even throws in a card with two weeks' pay in credit. Better than I expected, along with the days off. But something he said sticks in my mind.

"We did lose a few," I say, "but most of them should have made it out with me. They're fine on Martian air, so I assume they're back to work now. They're really the ones that got me out." What I think but don't say is that those bugs did more to save me than any of the fine company people up here in their high tower.

"I'm sure you remember from training—once a roach frenzies, it's never really the same again. We had to recycle the entire team that made it out with you. We'll be a little short-handed for a few weeks, but there's another batch coming up, new and improved, and we'll be back to full staff in no time at all." There's that smile again, and I'm struck with the image of a shark grinning as a meal swims by.

I nod, because I can't think of what else to do, and shake his hand. When I offer it, he can't refuse, and to his credit, he doesn't seem to want to. I guess I'm enough of a story now to make up for our difference in station. As I turn and head out of his office, back down the hall, and all the way down that elevator to the deep level where all the canaries sleep, I imagine him repeating my story at cocktail parties, embellishing where it suits him.

My quarters are quiet and dark, and I don't bother hitting the lights when I enter. I settle on the bed, where I must have slept ten hours after getting back from the cave-in. Before I drift off again, I drape my arm over the side and smile when I find the smooth blackness of Sam's shell. I pet him softly in the dark as he sniffs the blue marker I left for him and joins me in silent sleep.

About the Author

After living on every other American coast at least once, Ian Rose has settled into life in Portland, Oregon, where he works as a freelance web developer. A lifelong lover of the sea, he sets most of his writing in or on the ocean, but since there are currently none of those to be had on Mars, this story is an exception. Ian's work has recently appeared in *New Myths* and *Cast of Wonders*, and this is his second time appearing with Third Flatiron.

*****~~~~*****

For Sale: One Red Planet

by Jeff Hewitt

SMALL RED PLANET FOR SALE

Hello! Thanks for your interest in my listing. I'm selling the planet Mars, from the Sol System. It's, as I understand it, the last entirely private-held planet in that solar system. My family has owned it for generations, but when my grandfather passed away, it fell to me. Upkeep is too onerous for me at this time, as I live in another galactic cluster. It's just too far to do it justice.

As you may know, Mars is the fourth planet of the Sol system. It comes with two pristine moons. Interested parties should send a message to ECDTrimmond.44.265.XCLUSTER54552

>ECDTrimmond
XXXXXXMIKS<

Why's it red? Is there something wrong with the terraforming?

>XXXXXXMIKS
ECDTrimmond<

It hasn't been terraformed. Mars was held in trust for the last two thousand years. As I said, it's the last privately held planet in the system. It's pristine! A really good buy if you're familiar with Earth history at all.

>ECDTrimmond
XXXXXXMIKS<

Ehhhh, pass. Red's a terrible color for a planet.

>XXXXXXMIKS
ECDTrimmond<

Are you serious? You're not going to buy a planet because it's RED?

>ECDTrimmond
XXXXXXMIKS<

55

Yeah. Buyer's market. Nobody wants to terraform planets anymore. Good luck.

...

SMALL PLANET FOR SALE

Thank you for your interest. This listing is for a small planet in the Sol system. Pristine condition! Held in trust for over 2,000 years. Must see it to believe it! Can make a deal for special considerations. Contact:

>ECDTrimmond
MCONAQ9952411X<

That's a sparse listing. Does it come with any moons, and what are we looking at for gross mass and mineral distribution?

>MCONAQ9952411X
ECDTrimmond<

Two small moons. 6.4185 x 10^23 kg mass wise. Small, but like I said, pristine. Lots of nice iron oxide on the crust. Gives it a nice red shade.

>ECDTrimmond
MCONAQ9952411X<

Red planet, eh? Wouldn't happen to be Mars? We'll offer you 1.5 trillion. That's as high as I can go. It'll practically be a loss once we crush it down.

>MCONAQ9952411X
ECDTrimmond<

Whoa! You can't grind it down! There's historical significance. See attached:

ALL WHO MAY BE CONCERNED
FROM: INTERGALACTIC HISTORIC SOCIETY
RE: THE PLANET "MARS," SOL SYSTEM, MILKY WAY

In recognition of the place that Mars holds in the hearts of all Terrans, in recognition that Mars was humanity's first step beyond its moon, that the first colony was formed there, that the rest of the galaxy was greeted from its red surface, LET IT BE KNOWN that Mars shall always be respected and held IN TRUST by ALBERT TRIMMOND and his descendants, until such time that Sol itself burns out, destroying the rest of the system. Mars may be developed for the use of Humanity, as it has always done, but shall not:

1. Be gravitationally displaced

2. Transformed/terraformed other than to make it hospitable enough for permanent E-class colonies

3. Mined or exploited of resources to its detriment, or

4. Otherwise destroyed or removed before its natural time.

MCONAQ9952411X<
Ah, we see. No thanks, then.

...

PLANET OF HISTORICAL SIGNIFICANCE FOR SALE

One of the finest planets in the Sol System, birthplace of Humanity, is up for sale. Think of the history! Think of the prestige! Planet may be developed for human use as per the Intergalactic Historic Society, but must not be destroyed or heavily mined. Comes with moons! Perfect boarding and observation stations for those low-G experiments. Good size for a burgeoning clan of history-buffs, or anyone else with a taste for classics. Named after a Roman god. SERIOUS INQUIRIES ONLY

Contact:
>ECDTrimmond
TheBluxions<
Is it Jupiter?
>TheBluxions
ECDTrimmond<
No, it's Mars.
> ECDTrimmond
TheBluxions<

Oh. Thanks anyway.
>ECDTrimmond
IGRealEstate<

Hello >NAME HERE<! It's come to our attention you have toA PLANET< for sale/rent. As the largest firm in the galaxy, IGReal Estate would love to help you with your listing. Our team of experts
[DELETE]
>ECDTrimmond
Humans4HumansLeague<

Hi, I,'m a member of the H4H League, and we're very interested in your planet. It's got to be Mars, since that was the last planet held in human trust. What's your asking price? My name is Jerry.
> Humans4HumansLeague
ECDTrimmond<

Hi Jerry, thanks for your interest! It is, in fact, Mars. I was offered 1.5 trillion by a mining concern, but due to the historical significance obviously that was a no-go. Do you think your organization could do 1.5T? What exactly does the H4H League do?
>ECDTrimmond
Humans4HumansLeague<

That seems a fair price. I'm glad you asked about H4HL! We're a group of like-minded standard humans who wish to preserve and protect human history and culture. Did you know that many colonies now require their students to study the history of other species? Did you know that in one such classroom the children are required to pledge loyalty to alien gods? We at the H4HL think this is outrageous, and work to demand that human students are taught by humans, for humans. We reject the outside influence of galactic interlopers. Mars is of prime interest to us due to its historical influence and proximity to Earth. By the way, are there any squatters?
>Humans4HumansLeague
ECDTrimmond<

Ah. I see. Well, I can't argue with that. I think there's a small group of something or other in one of the many canyons. Let me take a look at the last surveyor report—yep, here it is. See attached:

SOL SURVEYING AND APPRAISAL COMPANY
MARS
2.24.4542
Centennial survey complete.
Atmosphere remains stable, smaller than 2% variance from last survey.
New impact crater, 25km in diameter, see attached.
Volcanic activity: 0.
Radiation: Background
Registered Population: 0
Unregistered population: 10.5 million (see attached census)
CENSUS
REGISTERED POPULATION
No Data Available
UNREGISTERED POPULATION
10,488,192 sapients
(Quadrupedal)
(Anaerobic)
Populations established in canyons LHRQ 135, 136, 122
Cities: 5
Unregistered population seems to be mainly made up of Iynains. Cities are well entrenched within cavern networks. Peaceful.
>ECDTrimmond
Humans4HumansLeague<
We can't share a human planet! Will the closing costs cover extermination fees?
>Humans4HumansLeague

ECDTrimmond<

Exterminators? You're going to kill the entire population?

>ECDTrimmond

Humans4HumansLeague<

It'll be our planet, what's it matter to you? You some kind of xeno-lover? Have one of those things ever helped you out? You probably don't even live in this cluster. Who cares? More than a hundred times those die every day across the universe.

>Humans4HumansLeague

ECDTrimmond<

Mars is not for sale to you or your ilk. Thank you anyway.

>ECDTrimmond

Humans4HumansLeague<

>WARNING THIS MESSAGE CONTAINS A MALICIOUS WETWARE PROGRAM! OPEN ANYWAY?<

[DELETE]

[User: Humans4HumansLeague placed on BLOCKED List]

Conversation [PLANET OF HISTORICAL SIGNIFICANCE Forwarded: GalacticPol]

...

SMALL PLANET FOR SALE IN SOL SYSTEM! RED! HISTORICAL! NO EXTERMINATIONS

Hello, and thank you for your interest. I recently inherited Mars, the last privately held planet in the Sol system, from my family trust. I live in a distant cluster and am unable to maintain it from so far away, and do not wish to go through that expense. The planet comes with two moons, and an official declaration of historical significance from the Intergalactic Historic Society, which allows light exploitation through mining, terraforming to establish up to class E colonies, and other, non-destructive, development.

This is a real chance to own a piece of human history! Think of the prestige! Please note: there is an established population of Iynains, around 10.5 million. They're mostly contained on one part of the planet. Part of the closing costs may cover peaceful relocation BUT NO EXTERMINATORS! This is important! Interested parties should contact:

>ECDTrimmond
AmbassadorGrimbdep<
Trimmond:

It came to my attention recently that you inherited our beloved Mars, which we knew to be held in private trust by a human party before now. I understand if your ire is raised in finding a group of squatters living on your planet. Before now, it seems, no one minded. I saw your posting and, with gratitude, note that you do not wish us exterminated. As you probably know, there are elements in the galaxy that are not welcoming of outsiders. We understand this. We also understand your desire to relocate our population contingent upon the sale of our planet. We do not wish for this, as many generations have grown up in the cool glow of your Sun. Many children have been raised in the caverns and cities that make up the canyons of your planet. It, to us, is a beautiful place. In light of this, and the fact that you want to sell it, would you consider gifting it to us, to be held in trust, maintained as per the Intergalactic Historic Society's declaration? You would be making a very large number of beings happy. Please consider this offer.

My humble thanks,
Grimbdep, Ambassador of Mars
>AmbassadorGrimbdep
ECDTrimmond<

Thank you for contacting me. That's lot of responsibility, and a helluva hard choice to make. I could have 1.5T credits to my name with the successful sale of the planet. That would take care of me and mine for a long time. Still, what right do I have to move so many people? How long have you been living on Mars?

>ECDTrimmond
AmbassadorGrimbdep<

Almost three hundred years, now. We came to Mars a lost people. We were expelled from our planet during a civil war. We did not come right to Mars; there were other planets where we stayed, but we were never welcome. When our ship finally brought us to this little corner of the galaxy, we were relieved to find what seemed to be the only undeveloped planet in the system. It was thought at the time that it remained undeveloped because no one from the other planets could use, or wanted, Mars. We settled out of the way. That is our story, simple as it is, difficult as it was.

>AmbassadorGrimbdep
ECDTrimmond<

May I have a few days to think about it? I have a family to consider.

>ECDTrimmond
AmbassadorGrimbdep<

Of course. We're your guests.

...

One Week Later

...

>AmbassadorGrimbdep
ECDTrimmond<

You may have Mars, with our blessing. There is only one condition. Do you have the ability and resources to construct human-friendly accommodations? We'd like to visit the new caretakers.

>ECDTrimmond
AmbassadorGrimbdep<

There are no words that describe the joy your news brought! The whole of our people celebrated your kindness and generosity. You will never be forgotten, and your children, your children's children, all your children until the end of all things will be welcome on Mars. We will begin building such facilities as soon as possible, and hope to see our benefactors soon.

...

Two Months Later

...

>ECDTrimmond
EarthMIL<

Mr. Trimmond, it's come to our attention through an anonymous tip that you recently sold Mars, a planet of prime strategic interest to Earth, to a group of non-human entities. . .

About the Author

Jeff Hewitt is a writer from North Georgia, where he works as a police dispatcher. *Redshifted* from Third Flatiron is his first appearance in print, though his works have been featured on the popular horror podcast *Pseudopod*, and the free online fantasy e-zine *Quantum Fairy Tales*. He's been writing since the first grade, and has self-published two novels, available from most online retailers.

Jeff lives with his wife Megan, who is finishing nursing school, and their three dogs: Sophie, a Pembroke Welsh Corgi, Beasley, a terrier, and Penny, a handful. You can find more information about Jeff and his work on his website www.jeffhewitt.net

*****~~~~~*****

Cadaver

by Robina Williams

"Wow! We got there!" The scientists in the control room at the Space Center whooped with joy as their probe touched down on the planet's surface after its 352-million-mile journey. For 253 days of nail-biting anxiety they had tracked the progress of Inquirer across the heavens. Now, they cheered and applauded, hugged and congratulated each other as the radio signals confirmed that the risky, expensive mission had been successful to date.

Stage one of the venture was over and had been a triumph. Time for stage two: the probe's investigation into the chemical makeup of the dead planet's terrain to try to establish whether organic life might have existed there in the past. It seemed unlikely, as previous exploratory landers had uncovered no sign of past geological activity, let alone any indication of there ever having been living matter; in fact they had sent back precious little information before falling silent.

However, it had been decided to make one further search. Crucial to this was the sharp-edged tool attached to the tip of Inquiry's arm; this knife-shaped piece of equipment was designed to slip through the layers of dust and sand on the surface, penetrate the stratum of rock beneath, and slice off samples for test and analysis in the onboard laboratory.

First, though, the probe needed time to settle itself in its new location in the arid bed of the crater that had been selected as its landing site, and orient itself toward the sun that would warm its outer plates and power it up. This, the watching scientists reckoned, should take a few days, and after the tension of the journey and descent, they could relax a little while waiting for the heat of the solar rays to fire up their precious artifact.

...

"Hey, you two, get back over here! We've work to do!" Lainin gestured and yelled to the figures sitting propped against a pile of boulders. "C'mon, guys! Break's over."

Raynor and Samlin heaved themselves to their feet.

Lainin gritted his teeth as he watched his charges plod toward him. *Keep your cool,* he told himself. *These lads aren't here out of choice.* Workfare! There was something to be said for it, for social and labor reasons, he supposed, but it wasn't much fun supervising folk who didn't really want to work. It was tough going trying to motivate the unmotivated. Still, these two were pleasant enough; they were good-natured, unlike some of the surly youngsters he'd had to endure the last few years. In fact he'd gotten quite fond of them during the weeks they'd spent together. He'd miss them when he was moved to a new team.

"Okay," he said briskly when the pair finally stood before him, "let's get on with it. Orders are to get this thing out of the way."

Raynor eyed the bulky form lying on the pebble-strewn ground. "Why can't it just stay here?" he asked. "It's dead. It's not doing any harm."

"Not now, maybe," Lainin agreed, "but what about when it decomposes? There could be all sorts of horrible stuff in its entrails. Alien bugs. . . who knows what?"

"Ugh!" With a grimace Samlin backed away. "It mightn't be safe for us to touch it, boss."

Lainin had been thinking much the same thought; still, orders were orders, and he had a work sheet to fill in. "It won't do us any harm, lad," he said, "provided the shell stays intact. Which it will."

Samlin still looked unhappy.

Cadaver

"Come on, Sam," Lainin urged cheerfully. "Sooner we get the job done, sooner we can pack up and go home for the night." Beckoning to the boys to line up beside him, he moved behind the six-legged creature and began to push. Between the three of them, they managed to roll it forward, over the gullies gouged out by the streams of brine that seasonally ran down the sides of the crater before rapidly drying up in the scorching heat of the sun. Muscular as they were, they were all sweating by the time they reached the entrance to the disused mineshaft that served as a landfill site, and they paused for a rest.

"So we're tipping it in whole?" Raynor asked.

Lainin nodded.

"Tip and run," Samlin said sourly. "We ought to get danger money for this job."

Again, Lainin reckoned Samlin wasn't far wrong. He shared the youngster's view that disposing of the corpse of whatever it was that had dropped into the crater was not a suitable task for them; to his mind the job should have been done by a specialist unit with specialist equipment, not by a general purpose team like his, whose only equipment was their muscles. On querying his orders he had been told to get on with it, as they were short-staffed. What, he had grumbled to himself, had happened to health and safety regulations? Stuff falling from the sky unnerved him. There'd been a fair bit of it coming down lately. This was the first time he had had to deal with it personally, and he hoped it would be his last.

"OK," he said when they had all regained their breath. "One big shove and it'll be over the edge. Then we'll chuck those rocks on top of it." He pointed to a heap of boulders close by.

"To stop it coming back up again?" Samlin asked, adding as Raynor grinned, "Well, we don't know what it is, do we? I mean, it just dropped out of the sky and—"

"Yes, yes," Lainin cut in. "Ready?" He moved round to the front to try to help maneuver the stiff body up to the mouth of the shaft. It was not an easy task, and he grabbed hold of the outstretched arm as he struggled to position the cadaver so that it would topple into the hole. "Heave-ho!" he cried, and they tipped it in.

As it dropped to its resting place, they stood listening to the sound of its falling as it struck the rocky sides of the shaft. Finally they heard a series of crackings as it crashed to a halt.

"Shell's broken, from the sound of it," Raynor commented. He joined Samlin and Lainin in the task of rolling the boulders to the shaft and pushing them in.

With a clatter, and more splintering sounds, the rocks landed on top of the dead alien.

"That's enough," Lainin announced. "It should be covered by now. Thanks, lads."

"You're bleeding, boss." Samlin pointed to Lainin's arm.

Lainin looked down. "Must have cut it on that damned thing," he muttered.

"You should get it seen to."

...

Not long after they had left the area, a dust devil whipped across the area, spinning along with such force that it obliterated the marks gouged out where the alien had landed; after the whirlwind had passed, no trace of its arrival or of any activity in the crater remained.

...

"Where's it gone?" the scientists at the Space Center asked each other frantically. They scanned the information they already had, examined from every angle the images transmitted from the probe, went back over every detail. They checked, rechecked, then checked again: the probe had descended successfully to the planet's surface, coming down in the crater that had been selected as its landing site, dropping onto a flat stretch not far from a cluster of boulders. It had performed beautifully, justifying the billions of dollars expended on it, to the jubilation and relief of the scientific team at the Space Center. Now it had vanished into thin air, leaving not the slightest trace. Conspiracy theories soon sprang up, of course, most of them featuring little green men hauling the probe away—but to where? And shouldn't some tracks be visible? And anyway, little green men—little green anythings—didn't exist, did they?

"It could have disintegrated," someone suggested.

"It could have," someone else agreed, "but it can't have dematerialized."

"So where is it, then?"

"We're looking in the right place, I take it?"

The charts and images indicated that indeed they were.

The assembled scientists fell into a baffled and worried silence. Their probe had disappeared, and with it billions of taxpayer dollars.

...

Lainin did not get his arm seen to immediately, though it began to hurt. Never one to make a fuss, he ignored the pain and went to work each day. When the cut failed to heal and began to weep, he put a dressing on it and bandaged the arm. The arm grew more painful, though, and stiffened. Samlin and Raynor noticed that Lainin was struggling. "You don't look too good, boss," Samlin said. "You should see a doctor."

"I'm okay, thanks," Lainin said. "I can manage." But he wasn't okay, and he wasn't managing. "Sorry, boys," he said a couple of days later when he had to sit down and rest. "Just need a break."

"Come on, Sam," Raynor said, "give us a hand— we're taking him back. He's not well."

"I'll be fine in a jiffy," Lainin said. "Just a bit tired."

"You're more than tired, boss," Raynor said. "You're ill. Anyone can see that." Ignoring Lainin's protests, he and Samlin helped their supervisor out of the crater.

"I do feel a bit off-color," Lainin admitted to the nurse at the company medical center.

"You look all out," she said, concerned. She unwound the bandage and gently eased away the dressing, grimacing as she saw the wound. "That's nasty! What happened?"

"I got a cut when I was moving that cadaver. I must have gotten some dirt in it, and it's gone septic."

The nurse put on a fresh dressing, rebandaged the arm, then picked up a syringe. "Hold out your other arm— I'll take some blood while you're here. And I'm making an appointment for you with the doctor for first thing in the morning. Now, can you get home on your own, or do you want some help?"

Lainin insisted that he could manage, and he did— just about, though he slumped into a chair as soon as he arrived back.

In the morning he returned to the medical center. The physician tut-tutted when he exposed the wound. After applying a fresh dressing to it, he returned to his desk and studied his computer screen. "I've got the preliminary results from your blood test now. It's—" he paused "—all rather puzzling."

"What's wrong?" Lainin was feeling anxious now.

"I don't know," the doctor admitted. "The lab results are difficult to interpret. They're out of the normal range."

"Meaning what?"

"Meaning I need to have some more tests done." The doctor pushed back his chair and reached for a syringe. "Arm, please. The other one."

Lainin averted his eyes as the needle entered his vein and the blood sample bottle filled up. He was feeling sick now, though whether from worry or infection he could not tell.

70

"I'll get this off to Hematology," the doctor said. "And I'll give you a prescription for an antibiotic for you to pick up at the Pharmacy on your way out. Now, go home and stay home. Rest. I'll be in touch."

Two days later Lainin was back at the medical center. "We don't know what's going on," the physician admitted. "It may be some kind of bacterial infection."

"Is it serious?"

The doctor hesitated. "We need to look into it. You'll have to go into hospital for a few days."

"But I've got to get back to work," Lainin protested.

"No work for you, until we've got this cleared up."

"But—"

"But we can't clear it up until we know what it is. Now, go home, pack a small bag, and wait for the ambulance."

In hospital, Lainin was put on stronger antibiotics, but his wound, far from healing, turned green and gangrenous-looking, and the surrounding area became inflamed and swollen. He was in greater pain now, feverish and with a faster heart rate. Frightened but wanting to know the truth about his condition, he asked his doctors to tell him honestly what was wrong with him; they were, he realized, as baffled as he was. They could see the effects of the illness he was suffering from but could not identify it. "Your tissue is dying, but we don't know why," they confessed.

Though Lainin was exhausted now, he tried to stay awake, fearing his dreams, for when, despite his efforts, he drifted off he would find himself in a terrifying world in which armor-plated creatures dropped onto him from the sky; their sharp-angled carapaces cut him, and alien bacteria entered through his open wounds, colonizing him, breeding within him, overwhelming him.

Too weak to raise his head from his pillow, he listened to a group of doctors talking quietly at the foot of his bed. "Really nasty bug," he heard one of them say, "whatever it is."

"Very virulent," another agreed. "Resistant to everything we've tried so far."

"What's the next line of treatment?" a third voice asked as the group moved away.

Lainin dozed off again, but this time his dream was different. He was no longer alone but in a platoon, with Raynor and Samlin flanking him; further along were the doctors who had been treating him. This small military force stood facing a horde advancing across the dusty red plain. He stared at the enemy but could not pick out any distinguishing features: all he saw was a dark-colored mass moving steadily, relentlessly.

"We're gonna be slaughtered, boss," whimpered Raynor.

They're only kids, poor things. They've barely lived. Lainin wanted to put his arms around the boys' shoulders and reassure them that everything would be all right in the forthcoming battle, but he knew that it wouldn't be. "Hang in there," he muttered. *As if they had any choice.*

"At the ready!" the commander shouted. "Attack!"

The platoon marched forward, their firearms trained on the opposing army. The weapons, though, did not slow the steady progress.

Lainin could hear Samlin moaning beside him. Then he could no longer hear the youth's voice, for it was muted by an approaching roar as a fast-spinning dust devil rushed across the plain. He could no longer see or breathe as whirling particles blocked his vision and filled his nostrils. Lainin felt himself struggling to breathe. . . then his nightmare was over.

The battle of the bacteria continued after Lainin's death, and there could be no question as to the outcome, for Martian microbes had no natural defenses against the invaders; the alien organisms, spreading from the patient to the staff, traveled beyond the hospital walls, colonizing, killing.

In time, with their hosts gone, the invading pathogens themselves declined and died. The probe from Earth extinguished the very life it had been sent to search for.

When, many, many years later, the next lander touched down, it was onto a barren lump of rock swept clean by dust.

###

About the Author

Robina Williams is the author of the Quantum Cat fantasy series: *Jerome and the Seraph, Angelos,* and *Gaea,* all published as print and ebooks by Twilight Times Books. She was previously a freelance journalist, mainly writing features on real estate. She now writes short stories and flash fiction in addition to her Quantum Cat novels. Her web site is www.robinawilliams.com

*****~~~~*****

No Ravens On Mars

by Martin Clark

We are what we do, not what we remember

We'd been on Mars less than 48 hours and already the threat of violence was so strong you could practically taste it. Planet-fall had been at E.A. Poe base rather than Pioneer, only to find it was ill-equipped to handle the numbers of colonists involved. Being cooped up while they monitored how well we'd survived the journey had everyone on edge, and then some. There was very little privacy in "Edgar," let alone anywhere to hide.

Bain stood beside me at the window, gazing out at the panoramic view of desert and scattered boulders. His voice was a basso profundo growl. "Christ! Nineteen months in the fucking freezer for *this*? What the fuck was I thinking?"

What indeed. *Yes*, I understood the need for those best suited to manual tasks, but Bain and his like were no more than foul-mouthed roughnecks. Even the few women present fell into the "brash and trash" category, not that I was overly interested in female companionship. In terms of intellectual accomplishment I appeared to be in a minority of one.

However, Bain was a big man, imposing, and not someone to be antagonised. I adopted an emollient tone. "We're trail-blazers, Bain, the first to make the journey in suspended animation—opening the way for mass colonisation. Anyway, in terms of the memory loss we all appear to be suffering from, I've been assured that it's only a temporary side-effect."

But despite my apparent confidence I was deeply worried. Although I'd retained literary and linguistic skills, everything else was a complete blank. I wasn't even

75

sure my surname was "Cooks," as my jumpsuit proclaimed. I cleared my throat. "I also fail to understand what caused me to volunteer for this mission, but now that we're here, surely we're all in this together?"

He grunted, scratching at the bio-monitor on his arm. "Says you. Well, treating us like lepers doesn't bloody help. What's the matter, aren't we good enough for polite society or something?"

He had a point. After reviving us, the medical team and other base personnel had beat a retreat back to Pioneer, leaving only Eve Korvo—in the form of a telepresence hologram—to handle the "meet and greet." Most of the other colonists had taken an instant dislike to her.

I scratched my own arm in sympathy. "To be honest, I don't think they could risk opening the pods in front of the existing colonists, in case we were all drooling idiots. Better by far to have a nice, clean death in transit due to an unspecified technical failure."

Bain looked sideways at me, his eyes hard. "What, you think they offed some of us? Those who came out spaz?"

I shrugged. "All I'm saying is that despite the cramped conditions there are *far* more than fifty-two bunks available, if the closed-off modules are anything to go by. Anyway, this is just deep-sleep psychosis talking. I'm sure the Mars authorities have our best interests at heart."

He clenched fists the size of ham hocks. "Bastards! Well, don't think they're gonna push *me* around when we're all one big happy family. They got a security officer at Pioneer? Well, he can go fuck himself." He grinned, savage satisfaction in his eyes. "As far as I'm concerned, who really runs things is up for grabs. Savvy?"

Oh, I understood him, all right. For Bain and his kind, physical intimidation was a way of life, the currency of social interaction. Not for the first time I wondered just

76

how prepared the existing colonists were for this influx of new blood. I suppressed a shiver, managed a wan smile, and made my escape, leaving Bain as would-be master of all he surveyed.

The cafeteria was sparsely populated, but I sought the company of Judy and Francine anyway—a form of safety in numbers, if only for my benefit. They were a newly formed lesbian couple who found my lack of overt biceps and tattoos refreshing. My friendship with them had earned me the instant nickname "Dutch," although I didn't know why and felt too peeved to enquire further.

Judy ruffled my hair. "Let me guess, Dutch, just another shitty day in Paradise?"

I smoothed it back into place. "Bain is on edge. Well, more so than usual. I fear he may do something rash."

Francine snorted. "Rash? His kind are born with a short fuse. I heard tell he's hooked up with Helen Gaines, but screwing her doesn't seem to have taken the edge off. Maybe you should go bitch to your *little friend* about the lack of security. Again."

I sighed. "All of us have access to Eve, at any time. There's no good reason to ignore her."

"Well, maybe I don't like being treated like a child and told to play nice. We've done fuck-all since we got here, and I, for one, am getting mighty bored staring at four walls."

"Six." Judy was big on points scoring. "All the rooms are hexagonal."

Her partner scowled. "Clever bitch."

"Dozy cow."

"Ladies, please! We're all a little stressed at present. Why don't I approach Eve for an update and report back? I'm sure that knowing our intended roles will calm things down and raise morale, Hum?"

Francine inspected her fingernails. "You can be such a little toady at times, Dutch, you know that?"

Judy took her hand and kissed it. "Yeah, you run along. The smart money is on you as sanitation operative. As in ass kisser."

I stood and mock-bowed. "Catch you later, ladies." They flipped me off in unison and I turned away—harmony restored.

...

The double pressure doors leading to Command slid open as I approached. We were locked out of all base systems, but I considered that a wise precaution, given the intellectual capabilities of my fellow colonists. Miss Korvo presented as a woman in her late twenties with bobbed hair, wearing standard base overalls. Her holographic nature was obvious, probably deliberately so. She smiled. "Good afternoon, Dutch, what can I do for you today?"

I frowned. "Why call me that? Who's been talking to you?"

"I monitor everything that happens here. Don't worry though, your secrets are safe with me. In any event, the bestowal of nicknames as a function of social acceptance is of interest, insofar as it falls within the wider analysis of group dynamics. However, I don't think you came here to discuss that."

I smoothed back my hair—a nervous gesture, I know—and forced myself to smile in return. "The question of our roles once we've been integrated into the colony has been raised again. I believe that it would greatly enhance group solidarity if we could put a 'what' to the 'who,' don't you think?"

She inclined her head. "The memory loss you suffered in transit has proved to be far more severe than projected. Reversing that *tabula rasa* is a precise and delicate operation, one that requires the subject to be—"

"Yes, yes, I know all that. But try explaining it to the *lumpenproletariat* out there."

78

"My, but we are feeling superior today. What's wrong, is Bain getting under your skin?"

I snorted. "I'm beginning to think this period of isolation is some kind of bizarre experiment in social Darwinism. Tell me, is there a new name for government by intimidation, or are you happy with a good, old-fashioned tyranny? Because that's what you'll get if Bain and his kind aren't slapped down hard, and sooner rather than later."

"Touchy, touchy! Well, don't worry, the situation will be resolved shortly—within a few hours at most. Surely you can find something to do until then? Or at least find somewhere to hide?"

"So we're supposed to keep on doing what we're doing? Which is to say, nothing? What a surprise. And I don't appreciate the sarcasm, by the way. In fact I wish to register a formal complaint with Pioneer—no, make that the Extra-terrestrial Administration back on Earth. You could definitely do with an attitude check."

Eve laughed. "Pot, kettle, springs to mind, Dutch—but I'll take it under advisement. Now, was there anything else?"

I sniffed, smoothed back my hair, and left.

...

My real name is Georges Cooks, hinting at partial French ancestry, although I carry no trace of an accent. The living space allocated to me was a bunk with integral locker as you'd find aboard a train sleeping car or in a *kapuseru hoteru*. At least it had a roller blind so that I could shut out the sight—if not sound and smell—of my fellow colonists. I tried to relax, going over my few personal belongings. They shed no light on my recent past or intended future; a framed photograph of a woman in late middle age, a leather-bound bible with Matthew 5, 18 and Mark 9 torn out, and a Swiss Army knife with all the attachments snapped off save the tool used for removing stones from horses' hooves. Nothing I would exactly call useful, although I slid the knife into my pocket, seemingly on reflex. OK, so the woman was probably my mother, but the bible? *If thy eye offend thee, pluck it out.*

The sound of nearby sexual congress, or at least energetic masturbation, drove me from my temporary refuge. Edgar was a hub-and-spoke design, and I walked the outer ring corridor, going nowhere fast. The level of CCTV coverage in Edgar wouldn't have disgraced a medium-security prison back on Earth. Just knowing that I was being constantly watched made the back of my neck itch. I plodded on, counting the number of cameras keeping track of my progress.

And stopped.

There was a gap.

The ceiling-mounted pod ahead of me was showing a red "off-air" light, creating a surveillance blind spot in the curved corridor. A strange oversight, but even a base this size required continual maintenance, and it was apparently off-limits to repair crews during our tenure. My sense of relief in isolation was almost orgasmic.

I sat with my back against the outer wall, so as not to be reminded of what lay outside. The metal panels felt cool through my "E.A. Issue" jumpsuit. I relaxed, letting my gaze wander, feeling the tension ebb from my shoulders, lulled by the slow beat of ventilation fans. Seconds became minutes. A few fellow colonists went past, but none gave me a second glance.

Strange.

I noticed a distinct multi-panel area of the inner corridor wall, defined by marginally wider gaps between it and the surrounding sections. This would have been invisible to the casual passer-by, but to me it stood out like the entrance to a Pharaoh's tomb. I waited until there was no one in sight before standing and subjecting the wall to closer scrutiny. There were small scuff marks either side of the defined area, as if some narrow-bladed tool had been inserted between the gap and used as a lever.

I had something that would serve just as well.

Under pressure from my knife a section of panels eased forward, sliding out on telescopic struts to stand proud of the wall. A fibre optic cable was twisted around one strut, pulled free from its intended socket, explaining the dead CCTV pod.

I looked behind the panels—and down a short maintenance tunnel ending in a sealed pressure hatch. Curiosity and, I admit, a sense of devilry drove me inside. I pulled the section of wall back into place. Recessed lighting flickered into life, and several diagnostic screens came out of standby mode. I ignored them, my attention focused on the pressure hatch, which was dogged but not otherwise secured.

My breathing was rapid and shallow. I felt like the hero in a dimly remembered children's adventure tale, a memory from pre-adolescence that had escaped erasure. Despite the "Level One Bio-Containment Only Beyond This Point" warning sign, I seized the small central wheel lock. It turned easily, and the hatch opened with a hiss of overpressure, bringing an antiseptic tang that irritated my throat. I was bathed in the cool blue glow of a sterilisation field.

The chamber beyond was perhaps five metres wide, home to a woman lying in the invasive embrace of a critical care support nest. Perhaps "torso" would be a more accurate description, as she had lost both legs above the knee and her left arm in its entirety. I recognised a Syversen cranial interface rig, more commonly found in the hard-core virtual reality gaming community, and a brain-stem umbilical linking her to a computer port. This was taking life support to a whole new level.

Eve Korvo flickered into view next to the reclining figure. She didn't seem pleased to see me. "Close that hatch immediately! Your very presence poses a severe health risk to the subject. Leave *now,* and I may overlook this unauthorised access."

I'm quite analytical, dispassionate even, and I often have trouble reading people—but I know bluster when I hear it. So instead of retreating I stepped through the hatch and closed it behind me. My ears popped as the pressure built up, and I felt suddenly light-headed, probably due to an oxygen-rich atmosphere. I smiled. "That's you lying there, Miss Korvo, isn't it? I can see the resemblance, although there isn't much of your real face left to make a comparison. It must have been one hell of an accident, but I see they've put what remains of you to good use. I take it that out here its a case of waste not, want not?"

She appeared close to tears, although some part of me wondered if the hologramic projection system supported that. "Get out! Get out! Get out, or I'll call security!"

I smiled. "And it's only a three-hour drive from Pioneer. Look, I'm not doing anything wrong. I just want us to get acquainted, nothing more."

Eve seemed to pull herself together and even attempted a smile. "I— I appreciate the gesture but, really, I'd much rather be on my own. I'm not comfortable with anyone other than the medical team seeing me like this. Look, Dutch, if you leave now, I'll make sure you become deputy to Director Sloan himself. A position well suited to your obvious intellectual abilities."

I let my smile slip away. "That was *far* too obvious, if you don't mind me saying so. You should have started small, offering something in basic administration, and worked up to a Control-level position if I proved difficult. So you're lying, and that means you have something to hide." I gestured around the chamber, "Something beyond all *this,* at any rate."

She glared at me. "I don't have to justify myself to the likes of—" and broke off, suddenly, biting her hologramic lip.

My voice remained calm. "The likes of what, Eve? Oh, they're a rough lot out there, and not my first choice to populate this brave new world of ours, but—"

"Criminals." She took a deep breath. "*Murderers*, every last one of you, even the women. You've all been condemned to death, and in each case the appeals process has been exhausted."

The chamber suddenly felt very cold. "Murderers? Some of the others, like Bain, I can well believe, but you're mistaken about me, Eve. My presence here is obviously an administration error, a terrible, ghastly mistake."

Eve sneered at me. "You? You're the worst—a serial killer, a high-functioning sociopath who planned his murders in exquisite detail. The others may have acted out of greed, envy, or lust, but *you* killed simply to see if you could get away with it, to see if you were cleverer than everyone else. I'm sickened to be part of the same species."

"But we still make for useful guinea pigs, is that it? Was that the deal? A memory wipe and experimental freezing in return for a full pardon?" I laughed, bitterly, and shook my head. "Mars as the new Botany Bay?"

"Don't be so naïve. Do you *really* think society would countenance fouling the high frontier with the likes of you? Don't you get it, Dutch, really? Someone as clever as you? E. A. Poe base, or, to give it its proper title, Extra-terrestrial Administration, Place of Execution."

I stared at her. "Fifty-two people? You'd kill fifty-two people, just like that?"

"We terminated those who didn't survive the journey intact. Your time here is just to check for any residual side effects. Once our studies are complete, I'll simply reduce the oxygen content and—" Eve broke off, realising she'd gone too far—*way* too far—in the presence of a serial killer.

83

But for the moment I ignored her, as my mind worked the angles. Eve ran the base, but I figured that in the event of her incapacity all critical systems would continue working in autonomous mode. If she went off-air, then Pioneer would send a team to investigate, although they'd have no reason to suspect foul play, given that she was hidden away like the Prisoner of Zenda. Bain and his buddies could easily deal with a technical crew, and they'd just as easily pressure a survivor into driving us back. The crawler could hold twenty, maybe even thirty of us at a push. Pioneer base wouldn't know what hit it.

Once we controlled Mars I couldn't see the E.A. stuffed shirts pissing away a multi-trillion dollar investment just to make a point, especially if we held hostages. The prospect of diplomacy never appeared so appealing.

I stepped forward and tore the brain-stem umbilical from Eve's skull, severing her control of all base systems. She stared at me, aghast. "Stop! Don't do this! Leaving me here like this, it's no better than being buried alive!"

There was no room for sentiment when I had a jail break to organise. I yanked the Syversen headset free, and the hologram Eve flickered out of existence.

Well, fuck her, there's no ravens on Mars.

About the Author

Martin Clark is a freelance writer and occasional poet. He contributes to several online publications, primarily Mythaxis.co.uk. His range of subject matter includes science fiction, urban fantasy, romance, and westerns. He puts this down to the somewhat eclectic mobile lending library where he grew up. He is author of

The Dead Don't Weep series currently being published by Eggplant Literary Productions.

Clark works as a local government officer in south-west Scotland and is also an evil stepfather.

*****~~~~~*****

The FALCON

by Jaimie M. Engle

Sokoloff knew he had a problem when the Rover started spitting out nothing but rock. He stepped out of the cab, crawling along the grate to the front grill of the massive sixteen metric ton machine, and opened the engine panel. No steam. No sparks. No flames. That was good. Compressing the node behind his left ear, Sokoloff said, "Computer, full diagnostic on Rover, bravo one-two-three-sixty."

The computer transmitted data over the chip embedded beneath his skin, which was processed and displayed on the 3-D screen before his left eye.

"Great," he said. "Cylinder's blown. That'll take all day."

In the distance, a towering wall of black clouds rolled closer. Lightning exploded in brilliant red and gold flashes. Sokoloff realized he didn't have all day. He returned to the Rover's cab and swiped a comm screen onto the dash. A blonde android appeared onscreen, wearing a navy blue coverall and cap bearing the Polzin Industries emblem. She was the next generation of FALCON, or Flexible Automaton Link-Controlled Offline Nanobots, the innovation that put Polzin on the map. A pioneering program of AI androids that could navigate nanobots without any human assistance; and like the ancient Egyptian hieroglyphs depicted falcons as gods, these robotic *gods* controlled most of the operations on the Mars base.

"FALCON, the Rover's bad. Probably got some Mars dust in the gears and blew a cylinder."

"Sending Ana," she replied, before the screen disappeared.

Near the end of the 21st century, uranium sources neared depletion on earth. Polzin Industries, in conjunction with the UN, sent cosmonauts to Mars to mine marsconium, a clean consumable energy source found deep in the planet's core. Sokoloff had immediately volunteered to oversee the FALCON operations. He and his crew had stayed on the transport ship for several months, while nanobots built an enviro-dome 150 kilometers high covering over 90 kilometers of Mars's red surface.

With a manufactured environment similar to Earth's, the cosmonauts could work within the dome without the bulk of spacesuits and helmets. Mining was the same here as it was on Earth—tedious, dangerous, and requiring split-second decisions and maneuvering capabilities, which meant the difference between life and death. Only a few months into the mission, a marsconium deposit was discovered hundreds of meters deep. And after three years, Sokoloff was still mining that find.

But at night, when it was quiet, Sokoloff thought of Milana.

While he waited for the repair module, Sokoloff sat back in the Rover's pilot seat and took out a flask. He gulped a hot mouthful of the spirits and grimaced. Alcohol on the Mars base was illegal, but the same machinery used to distill his water worked fine to make his drink.

After half an hour, Ana rolled up, churning red dust behind. Rock crunched beneath the tread of her tank wheels as she approached and parked. A highly advanced nanobots repair system, Ana could do things and get in places that no human being ever could. Sokoloff put away his flask and got back to work.

"Hello, baby." He opened Ana's hatch and pulled out a length of tubing. Pressing the node behind his ear again, he said, "FALCON, initialize diagnostics and repairs on Rover, bravo one-two-three-sixty."

"Initializing."

Hundreds of thousands of flea-sized robots burst from the tubing and attached to the Rover to perform diagnostic checks. The information was relayed between them in a millionth of a second as the nanobots worked with the precision and unity of an army of ants.

"Rover clear," announced the FALCON. "Checking shaft."

Moving as one living organism, the nanobots sped down the 800-meter shaft to check the rest of the Rover's components.

The raging storm beat on the curved walls of the dome. In three years, he had never seen a storm this fierce. Luckily, he was the only human left on this rock, unless you counted humanoid robots. The storm season on Mars lasted six weeks, with a replacement crew due to arrive at the season's end, less than a week away. Although he was petitioned to evacuate, Sokoloff refused to abandon Ana.

Not like he had Milana.

The dome shook violently. Something wasn't right. Sokoloff rushed back to the Rover's cab and cued up the comm screen. "What's going on?" he asked the FALCON. He'd forget she was an android sometimes, her anthropomimetic features set in perfect proportion.

"Electromagnetic storm. Category eleven. Sustained winds at four hundred and sixty kilometers."

"Are you sure?"

"I have not been programmed with opinions."

Sokoloff ran his fingers through his black hair. Lightning strobed above the dome spindling down the curved lens like fire-rain.

"Probability of dome survival, eighteen percent."

"Eighteen percent? That can't be right. Get a message to Dr. Polzin that—"

"Communication with Earth is not possible. Advise immediate return to the ship."

Sokoloff shook his head. "I can't do that. Ana's down the shaft."

89

"Survival probability dropping eleven point two percent every minute. Ana's survival probability remains at one-hundred percent."

Sokoloff swore under his breath as he jumped into the cab of the Rover. He turned over the engine and forced the gears into place. As he drove away, he saw a flicker of Milana's face, and he swore he saw one of the nanobots shoot out of the shaft. Ana wanted his attention. She didn't want him to go.

"I'm not leaving her," he said through gritted teeth, then slid the holographic screen across the dash until the FALCON disappeared.

Sokoloff jumped out of the rover and ran back toward the shaft. The dome rattled as the winds tore at it like an above-ground earthquake, until with a deafening crack, a weak joint in the dome collapsed, then split open. The gale flooded into the fissure at an alarming rate. Sokoloff's pulse raced. He dove into the back of the Rover and strapped on an oxygen mask. The doors hissed closed, sealing him in, and he grabbed the emergency suit from the rear, quickly stripping down to his undergarments to put it on. The tight reflective suit fit like a second skin. The Rover suddenly bucked. Sokoloff looked out the window.

"Oh, my God."

The dome peeled back and scrolled at the edges.

Ana was still out there.

Sokoloff put on his helmet. He switched the comm link to manual using the buttons on the forearm of his suit. "FALCON," he said. "Send Ana up."

"Negative," the FALCON replied. "Diagnostics are not complete."

A chill stopped Sokoloff dead in his tracks. Ana had never disregarded his commands before. Shuffling back into the cab, he shouted, "Abort! Abort! Send Ana up, now!"

Lightning sliced through the air with a crack. Blinding light filled Sokoloff's visor. The hairs on the back of his neck stood on end. Reaching for the door panel, he repeated, "Abort diagnostics!"

"No."

No? How could that be possible? "Did you say, 'no?'" Sokoloff asked, dumbfounded.

"Diagnostics are seventy-three percent complete. Abort impossible."

Sokoloff's body tingled as the color drained from his face. What was happening? Why was the FALCON not taking orders? Had its programming been fried?

The storm.

The electromagnetism of the Mars lightning must be disturbing the android's inner workings, rebooting her. He would need to override the system manually, which meant he had to go out in the storm. He had to get to Ana. He couldn't leave her to be destroyed by something outside her control.

Not like he had Milana.

He slid open the cab door, his boots skidding across the steel grate, and pressed through the blinding copper dust toward the mobile mainframe encased in a steel cage several yards away.

Milana had been six years old when the cancer hit. He had prayed, begging God to take him instead of his little girl. When God didn't cure her, Sokoloff had worked for a cure of his own, finding a way to get nanobots into his daughter's bloodstream to attack and destroy the cancer cells. Millions of nanobots acting as little gods were mixed with his own DNA to make the autonomous robots organic, allowing the biomimetrics to pick up where her own blood cells had failed. Ana.

He and Ana would fight the cancer with her.

Reaching the mainframe, he forced the steel doors open, and punched in abort codes on the panel to stop the FALCON and save Ana.

"Stop!" the FALCON fired through his headset. "Stop!"

Somehow when Ana had been inside of Milana, Milana's DNA had merged with the nanobots, and although Ana hadn't succeeded, and Milana had succumbed to the cancer, a piece of her still lived inside Ana's core. Tears slipped down Sokoloff's cheeks.

He could still save her.

The thunderous quake preceded the swarm of nanobots funneling up the shaft and out onto the surface like hungry locusts. As one, they charged Sokoloff, knocking him onto his back and blanketing his suit, tearing away at the pliable metal shrouding his body, and invading his helmet to embed into his skin. One by one, Ana ate through his flesh, devouring his muscles to enter his bloodstream; millions of machines moving under the FALCON's command.

He remembered Milana's face before she became sick, that summer at the beach house when they held hands and played in the surf. The sun glinted off her blonde hair, the same shade as her mother's. He'd postponed his trip to Mars when Milana got sick, and he'd told her many stories about the Red Planet.

"Daddy, will you take me to Mars someday?"

If she only knew.

Her laughter echoed in his ears, as Ana consumed his whole being, the FALCON infiltrating his body and mind, fully controlling him.

"I love you, daddy," Milana had said, holding him tight. "Promise me we'll be together forever."

And as Sokoloff heard the FALCON say, "Diagnostics complete," his body no longer under his control, his soul permanently imprisoned behind his mind, he could finally fulfill his promise to his daughter.

They *would* be together forever.

###

About the Author

Jaimie Engle has run a body shop, managed a hip-hop band, modeled bikinis, and danced at the Aloha Bowl halftime show. This wife and mother of two currently tutors in creative and essay writing, and offers a manuscript critique service for aspiring authors. She has published many short stories online and in print, including *Writer's Digest* and a children's piece appearing in *Clubhouse Jr.* in 2014. She was awarded honorable mention in L. Ron Hubbard's Writers of the Future contest in 2013 and second place in the 2012 Space Coast Writer's Guild's short story competition. Her debut middle grade novel, *CLIFTON CHASE AND THE ARROW OF LIGHT,* is available through Amazon and her website. Drop in on her at www.jaimiengle.com to read some of her short tales.

*****~~~~~*****

First Step

by Jason Lairamore

"I'm here to help," Jeremiah Martins said to the frowning, unshaven face of the man once he'd reached the other side of the little airlock.

The water collector habitat was one of many built in the northern latitudes of Mars. Usual habitats had about ten to twelve people. This one had only two, a man and a woman, perfect for his purposes.

The woman clutched the man's arm, her eyes red, and her face white. She was obviously in shock.

"Can you get us out of here? Can we leave?!" She nodded, and spittle flew from her mouth. When Jeremiah didn't answer right away, she turned her intensity to the man. "Herb, tell him to take us away."

Herb, the man's name was Herb. Jeremiah had never heard that one before. He liked the strong sound of its single syllable.

"We killed the cat a few days back to give us an extra couple hours," Herb said and shrugged. He acted like a man who'd already tossed his care away. Jeremiah had seen that so often. He continued to wonder why people always drifted to either end of the spectrum when faced with a most certain death.

"Where's your system housing?" he asked. He'd learned over the years he'd been doing this to never mention the specific problem that was the cause of their imminent death. Emotional responses to the specific label associated with their death were never positive. He'd had close calls from poorly chosen words in the past.

Herb sidestepped and sat down next to a single electric heater. The entire dome had been sealed up tight, except for the tiny little living area Herb and the woman shared. They were trying to save as much air as possible.

Herb used his free arm to point to the rear of the operation space. The woman jerked at the mere point he gave toward the source of their problem.

"I'm scared, Herb," she said hoarsely. Herb rocked her back and forth. She closed her eyes tight, and fresh tears fell from her eyes.

"It's okay, Ida," Herb said. "Everything is going to be okay."

Jeremiah squeezed by them and took the few steps to reach the secondary airlock. The dense plastic was blackened from the outside, most likely from some kind of chemical reaction, maybe a fire. He couldn't see a thing of the outside from the inside, which was good. He wouldn't have to play any misdirection tricks this time.

He made sure his suit was secure, just to keep up appearances. The habit was a good one to keep. It wouldn't do to scare anybody. He'd done that in the past, and it'd never ended well.

He cycled through the lock to the region beyond.

Herb and Ida's problem could have been condensation in the wrong place, or a sudden freeze, or just the right amount of wind and heavy dust. Whichever the case, it didn't matter. Though he knew the tech sitting before him, and how to fix it right up, he didn't mess with the repairs. It was all substandard stuff. Instead, he tore out the old water collector tech and replaced it with better hardware. He did the same with the re-breathers, the waster recyclers, and the soil biotic composer. He fixed it all, and made it better.

His help done, he cycled through the lock. Herb and Ida were still huddled by the heater. Neither of them looked up at him as he took the few steps to the outer airlock. They were most likely guarding themselves from seeing what they assumed would be pity in his eyes.

He stepped into the little airlock that led outside and pulled the door almost closed.

"You're all set," he said. "Herb, Ida, you are going to be very wealthy. Enjoy your retirement." They'd make a hefty sum from the patents of the tech he'd left them.

He shut the door and hit the cycle button as Herb started to look up.

It was time to move on.

...

Moving was always hazardous. But that was the only way to get what needed done, done. As he picked up some speed in his single-seat buggy, he scanned for another job. He should be able to get one more done before lying low. One more, then he would stop moving for a while so that the dust might settle. Too much stirred up dust was not a good thing, especially on Mars.

He found a job right away and shook his head. Jobs shouldn't be this easy to find, not here, not on Mars. These people were supposed to be the best and brightest.

This next one was a rarity. He'd seen only one like it before, and he hadn't liked how it'd turned out. He tried to cancel the incoming signal so he could search out another, but it was too late. He ended up cranking the buggy in the indicated direction.

He couldn't say no. A life was at stake.

He checked the site location and settled in for a long drive from the ice. This next job, the last before a break, was down near the Valles Marineris. It was close to some of the denser settled areas—closer than he liked, anyway. It was but one more thing he'd have to deal with.

...

After more hours than he cared to keep track of, where he drove all over Mars's red, rocky potential, he finally arrived. The habitat was a greenhouse in the bottom of the valley. It was a research and development outpost, a workstation where they grew microbes and developed Earth dirt.

He took a care to keep his motions slow as he entered the locks. The girl inside probably wouldn't appreciate any sudden motions on his part.

The building was a steaming mass of greenery that filled up either wall. The path down the center was narrow, and made more so by the continuous chemistry lab set-up that ran down the entire length of the building.

He did not see the girl he sought right off.

"Don't try to stop me," she said from somewhere deeper in the mass of leaves. Her words were slurred.

Jeremiah didn't respond. To do so would have only frightened her. He edged closer and closer, until finally, he saw her.

She was 168 centimeters of curves and curly brown hair. The under-suit elastic she wore really brought out the beauty of her many fine features.

As he saw her, so she saw him. She caught her breath and snatched up a full vial of some liquid. It was what she'd been bent over working on at the time of his arrival.

Her features were very finely balanced. Her green eyes glowed with fire.

Jeremiah held up his hands, palms up, as a sign of peace.

"Who are you?" she asked in a slur.

"Jeremiah," he said. "I am here to help."

She smiled, showing perfect white teeth. "How'd you know I needed help, Jeremiah?"

He took a closer look at the compounds she'd been working on. It was some sort of methane fertilizer derivative, meaning either a bomb, or poison.

The airlock cycled open at his back. The girl's smile grew wider. He didn't like the change of intensity in her eye.

"Maribel, don't you do anything stupid, you hear," a man said. He sounded as drunk as the girl.

"I'm going to do it, Travis!" she called. "You come any closer I'll blow you up with me."

Jeremiah positioned himself so he could see both the girl and the approaching man. Inebriants were hard enough to deal with, but to add to that a suicidal beauty holding a supposed bomb, and her probable lover who she had most likely been recently fighting with. . .

"Who's this?" the guy said as soon as he saw Jeremiah standing there with his hands up and empty.

"He's here to help, Travis," Maribel said. "Maybe he likes me, like you like Kate."

Jeremiah shook his head at Travis. "I'm only here to. . . "

"Kate was a mistake," Travis said over him. "And it was ages ago. We were stuck in that sandstorm for days. I thought I was going to die."

"The soil work here is of vital importance for the generations to come," Jeremiah interjected. Neither of them paid him the least bit of attention.

"Well, it's too late," Maribel said. "This vial is going to blow. And there is nothing you can do about it. It's your fault. Now you really are going to die."

Jeremiah didn't waste another second. He grabbed the vial as quick as lightning and vaulted to the exit before either of the two crazy drunks could process what he'd done. He made it out of the greenhouse and a full ten meters away before the vial in his hands erupted and everything turned to white noise.

...

His senses came back after his body. It was an odd feeling to wake to his body thrashing about.

"That thing's alive!" somebody said. The voice was muffled, but he could tell it was the girl from the greenhouse.

"Glad I put it in that transport box now, aren't you?" That was the man, Travis. Neither of them seemed the least bit drunk anymore.

He relaxed what was left of his body and felt a steady vibration thrum through the sealed box he was in. They were taking him somewhere, and he couldn't tell where, not while in the sealed up box. These boxes were built to resist any and all solar and cosmic radiation.

A sudden realization almost made him start back up his useless thrashing. He could die in here. Half of his body had already turned to vapor and sand. What was left was mostly inert, and it would stay that way without the rays that constantly fed Mars's surface.

There was no way to escape. He couldn't shift. He couldn't disseminate at all.

"Where are you taking me?" he asked. It was lucky that he'd kept his vocals in the explosion.

"The only place we can take an alien," the girl said. She sounded happy. "You're going to make us rich and famous. You weren't lying when you said you were here to help."

They both laughed. Jeremiah relaxed. He'd get out of the box soon enough. They'd have to show his mangled body to somebody sooner or later.

...

It took a long time to get where they were going. More of his body had decayed into nothing by the time they got there.

The box he was in was moved from the vehicle and was placed on a cart of some sort. They moved for a while, then he felt the pressure differential of an airlock. After that, the trip was almost smooth.

"Its blood is black, just like the rumors, sir," he heard Travis say once they'd finally stopped.

"And the flesh is fibrous, and purple," Maribel added. "It turns to sand when it is removed."

The seals popped on the box, and Jeremiah smiled. The lid was lifted free. Jeremiah relished the feeling as the sweet nutrients poured into his waiting receivers. The flow was a mere trickle, to be sure, as they were within a controlled environment. But it was so much more than the nothing he'd been getting while in the box.

He was pulled from the box and made to stand. He maintained the position only through tremendous effort. He used some energy to bolster his hips, knees, and ankles. He would have a need of them very soon.

His upper body and torso hadn't fared so well. One whole arm was gone, as were most of the pseudo-organs and soft tissue of his abdomen. He was acutely aware of his naked vertebrae and spine. It was barely functioning to keep his center of gravity balanced. He did what he could internally to strengthen it, but left outward expressions alone.

He didn't want them to know of his ability. They weren't ready.

"Why do you look human?" a new voice asked. It was then that he realized that the explosion had taken his eyes. He used just enough energy to correct the issue without drawing attention.

"Rumor is they are shape shifters," Travis said. "That's why we haven't caught one before."

"I was asking the creature."

The man speaking was one of three people sitting behind an official looking table. These three were the ruling body on Mars. That meant he was within the caves of Arsia Mons, the primary human site.

A woman sat to the right of the man. She looked him up and down with wide-eyed wonder. Another woman, to the man's left, was frowning.

"We need answers," the frowning one said.

"Let me go," Jeremiah answered.

The man's smile was condescending. The woman with wonder in her eyes just kept shaking her head.

"We can't let you leave," she said. "You're too important."

He'd had some time to think about how he'd respond to the obvious answer to his command, and so had been fashioning just the device needed for some time.

With the only hand he had left, he pulled a square piece of metal from his pocket and stuck its adhesive backing to his chest. Then he pushed the box's singular button. A two-minute timer started ticking down.

Maribel wasn't the only one who could make a bomb.

"Scan it if you like," he said, "but it's real. Let me go, or you all die."

The man in the middle lost his smirking demeanor. The frowning lady kept on frowning. The lady of wonder just looked more excited than ever.

"It's bluffing," Maribel said. She positioned herself before him, her furious beauty on full display. "It's here to help us. It sacrificed itself to save Travis and me. That's how we caught it in the first place."

He'd saved the greenhouse and the vital work on Earth soils. That had been worth more than a couple of drunks acting stupidly. Humans and their egos, it was something he still found hard to process.

"Let it go," the frowner said. The man beside her nodded and sighed. The wonder lady shook her head, but kept her mouth shut.

He'd known this ploy would work. He'd used the human's greatest weakness against themselves. Their weak mortality was his greatest tool.

They followed him in silence to the exit airlock. He cycled it open and stepped inside.

"Why are you here?" the lady with wonder in her eyes asked. "The advanced tech we've found, the odd formulas left in just the right place to help us progress. Why are you doing this?"

He looked at the gathering crowd, each in turn.

"Survive," he said. He found Maribel's eye and held it. "I am here to help."

102

...

He walked away as fast as he could, knowing they watched him. When the bomb reached zero his body vaporized. The planet's surface where he'd stood heated to glass.

He was no more.

Surely, they'd think him dead. There was no way they could have seen one of his great toes detach and burrow into the surface just before the explosion.

The toe wasn't much, but it was more than enough to start again. His work was far from finished.

He'd been put on Mars to wait, to see if Earth could make it here.

And it had.

They'd made their first step, the hardest step of all. His job was to see that they did not now fall, for they had greater travels to make, travels out amongst the stars. He must keep at his work. They had to be prepared for the exodus that was to come.

They needed to be ready.

###

About the Author

Jason Lairamore is a writer of science fiction, fantasy, and horror who lives in Oklahoma with his beautiful wife and their three monstrously marvelous children. He is a published finalist of the 2012 SQ Mag annual contest and the winner of the 2013 *Planetary Stories* flash fiction contest. His work is both featured and forthcoming in *The Blue Shift* magazine, *Postscripts to Darkness, Carnage: After the End Vol. 2*, Kerlak Publishing, Emby Press, Great Escapes, *Mad Scientist Journal*, and *Pantheon* magazine, to name but a few. You can find out more about Jason at http://www.facebook.com/#!/jason.lairamore

MarsMail

by Michael McGlade

Welcome to MarsMail your interstellar communication hub.

(changed from M-mail following a legal dispute from Gmail)

You're 18—congratulations! Your five years of state-mandated service begins today. Please use this interstellar flight from Earth to get to grips with your new life on Mars, make some friends, have fun.

As a new employee of MarsIndustries we value your drudgery. We know moving is stressful, and you probably have family back home you wish to communicate with, so we've taken the hassle out of interplanetary communication with MarsMail (all your mail is screened for increased user experience and tailored AdMail™). A welcome message in your inbox details your work assignment, dormitory location, and labor hours.

MarsIndustries—where mining the core of the planet is worth its weight in gold.

Latest updates and features of your interstellar MarsMail inbox:

AdWords

At the beginning of each email, you will find a brief ad specifically tailored to your message's content. Arranging a date with a co-worker? You'll find an ad for the nearest tapas bar, wine emporium, and scented candle store. Don't worry, we'll also inform your co-worker of the nearest Family Planning center. AdWords is easy, intuitive, and best of all it's free. Find and buy the things you actually want!

AdList

Action-item all those important tasks in our ad-driven to-do-list. Plan for the harsh climate, planetwide dust storms, and sulfuric acid rain caused by heavy industry. Need to get some shots? Learn to shoot a gun? Fight the resistance? MarsMail helps you do it all. With ads.

AdVance

Skip through the spam and trash folders, get right to the core. When you type something, we'll find it for you. Maybe you've mentioned it before in your mail? We've read everything you've written and received, so we know you better than you know yourself. We'll suggest exciting medical procedures, your new favorite foods, and traits and features for your genetically engineered offspring. Adverts for everything you ever wanted before you even knew you wanted it.

AdVice

We can detect from your tone and the pressure with which you strike the keys how stressed you are. We'll arrange for a government-regulated masseuse (only 1.2 miles away!) to book you in for an appointment. We'll also message everybody in your contact list to be extra nice to you.

AdApt

We've modified the new MarsMail for your specific requirements. No more will your friends need to stage an intervention because of increasing depression and substance abuse. We'll suggest a suitable psychiatric doctor (only 0.3 miles away!), a Rehad Center (only 1 miles away!) and pharmacist for your prescription of Prozac (only 10 feets away!). From next month, each referral you click on will earn you AdPoints, which you can redeem for even more great ads.

AdJust

It's never been easier: AdJust writes emails for you! Based on your previous email and Internet search history, AdJust will simply replicate your personality and writing style—but with ads, of course! (Helpful if you will be away from your laptop for a long period of time.) This way, you'll be able to keep in communication with your Earth family while you work the state-mandated requisite 23-hour daily shifts. Yes, OK, half your money will be taken in Mars taxes and a quarter for rent, gas, and air, but working long hours means you'll still take home more money than you'd get working 24-hour shifts on Earth. Plan what you'll do with your single hour of daily leisure time with AdList™.

AdDict

An enthusiastic devotee of a sport or pastime? We will page you every five seconds (can be set more frequently on the Settings page) during a sporting match to let you know what you could be buying. Maybe you'd like to know the current in-match betting odds? *Bam!* We pump it straight into your cerebral cortex. And to let you know we value your loyalty as a MarsMail user, we will periodically ask you to fill in a survey with your opinions on how we can improve our service. We won't act on your requests, but at least we pretend to listen, unlike Ymail.

A-dAy

Never trust an atom. They make up everything. Just our little joke. Expect something cute in your inbox every day from us, something to brighten up your day. Also, take some time to buy our products. Just click on the ad. It's right there at the top of your email.

AdDendum

MarsMail has exploded in popularity, which means that there are occasional server slowdowns and down times. Although MarsMail lets you keep your mail archived on our server, don't count on it being the only backup for important data. If your stuff goes missing, it's your own fault. What do you expect?—It's free!

AdIos, satisfied MarsMail user.

About the Author

Michael McGlade grew up in an Irish farmhouse where the leaky roof didn't bother him as much as the fear of electrocution from the nightly scramble for prime position beneath the chicken lamp, the only source of heating in the house—a large infrared heat lamp more commonly used for poultry. His seminal influences were Darwin's Survival Of The Fattest and a morbid belief that "undying love" meant you had a soft-spot for zombies. Never allowing these misapprehensions to hold him back from success, he understood that nothing is as clear as the illegible comprehensibility of the modern world.

His short fiction has been published in *Jupiter Science Fiction, Green Door, Grain, OMDB Mystery*, and other journals. He holds a Master's degree in English from Queen's University, Ireland. You can find out the latest news and views from him on McGladeWriting.com.

*****~~~~~*****

And A Pebble in Her Shoe

by Kara Race-Moore

One small step, she thought, *just one more small step.*

Navya knew the only way to live was to lie and lie and lie again. As many lies as it took to convince herself to keep moving forward.

A gust of wind whipped around her, tugging at the folds of her Vera Wang bio-suit, as if begging her to stop and play. Navya spun in a tight circle, terrified the wind was the harbinger of another sandstorm, but all she saw was the same unending rocky surface. The horizon was split in two: the lower expanse the dull red of the ground and the upper half the pale orange of the sky. It was her wedding day, and Navya Patel was stranded in the middle of the Sinai Planum.

At the first wedding on Mars the bride and groom were photographed standing on top of Soffen Cliff, the Martian panorama and beginning of the colony laid out behind them, perfectly illustrating the mixture of old and new as the happy couple smiled for the camera. And now, a generation later, the tradition was that every couple about to marry was photographed on that cliff, the colony burgeoning in each nuptial portrait.

Navya braced herself as the ground slanted downwards, and she allowed the momentum to take her on a partial slide, partial hop, until the ground leveled off again. Every bit of energy she could save would get her that much closer to home before the rebreathers maxed out, before dehydration or hypothermia set in, or before another sandstorm managed to kill her.

The sensors had indicated that there was a sandstorm developing in the area, but the wedding pictures had to be taken so they could be sent to Earth on schedule for the spring bridal catalogs that were going to feature an article on the wedding of Navya Patel and Marijus Kalnietis. Everyone was sure there was enough time, old Dr. Calvin "Firststep" Fitzsimmons even joking that a sandstorm behind them would make for a better picture.

At least they had already taken several photos when the storm had blown up, she reflected. It would make for an especially poignant illustration to her obituary, sure to get more funds for the colony. Events like this—weddings, funerals, births—were all documented and sent Back Earth and used by their Earth-side members to drum up continued interest—and investors—in the colony.

When the sandstorm had taken a capricious turn and came charging directly towards their little bluff, her first thoughts had been to worry about the photos being sent out on time, rather than for her personal safety. It was a miracle she had survived. Her wedding dress, however, was in much worse condition than she was.

The outfit had been designed with one outdoor photo shoot in mind, rather than hikes across an inhospitable landscape. Unlike the bright blue of normal bio-suits, the wedding dress was, or rather, had been, dazzlingly bright white, meticulously cleaned after every wearing. Now, however, it was as pale red as the landscape, bedraggled, torn, and, Navya nervously suspected, beyond repair. Dying out here might be preferable to the angry reception she would get for ruining the colony's only wedding dress.

The dress was now old-fashioned, and there was debate on perhaps updating it to make it look more like Back Earth styles. True, it was constantly being modified to fit each bride that wore it, but it had been kept as the same layered and laced affair it had been when it had arrived.

It had been designed by Vera Wang LTD and sent up for the first wedding on Mars, with the caveat it would be shipped right back to be sold at auction for the fashion company's profit. Instead, the colonists had made a point to say on camera what a nice *gift* the wonderful fashion designers had sent them and wasn't it *nice* to provide them with a real wedding gown that would be shared amongst all the Mars brides and treasured *forever,* thank you *so* much.

And so, despite the fact there was a legal contract stating the dress was technically the property of Vera Wang LTD, in the face of what would have been a horrendous case of bad press, the elite fashion house had let it slide and graciously allowed the colonists to keep it, with the understanding that it was to stay community property. If it ever became private property, Vera Wang LTD would immediately send a seizure notice and demand its return.

So Navya was more than a little worried about people's reaction to showing up in the tattered remains of a cultural icon. Almost all of the lace had been torn away in the storm, leaving it stripped down to the basic bio-suit design, although some of the useless swags of silk still clung to her thighs and hips. Navya cursed the Vera Wang designers for putting so much useless ornamentation on the outfit and neglecting something as basic as a radio. She clenched her gloved fists in useless frustration.

The gloves were still see-through, despite the dust. They had been designed to be as flexible and clear as the then-current latest technology would allow, which, even today, was still an impressive feat of textile engineering. This way the ring finger was visible in all photo shoots.

Navya could see her ring, a little spark of hope that she might still live to take it off and have Marijus put it on again during the ceremony. Engagement rings were an extravagant Earth custom that had to be left behind, but, exchanging the traditional gold for the local hematite, the wedding band was still part of the ceremonies.

Navya and Marijus' wedding wasn't going be as big a deal as Anne and Brad's wedding last year. Anne Kennedy had been the first baby born on Mars. Not, of course, the first fetus conceived on Mars, but the first one carried to term, and that meant something too, even if Anne wasn't a whole chapter in most law texts these days on abortion rights. Brad had been born a month after.

Anne and Brad's marriage had practically been arranged in the cradle. Not that anyone had been sold for some goats, like Back Earth's olden days, or anything crazy like that—it was just expected of them, for the good of the colony.

For the good of the colony. The phrase tended to be the answer to everything, said so often and so rapidly by exasperated parents to whining children that it tended to come out all as one word: forthegoodofthecolony.

And so, for love and the good of the colony, Anne and Brad had married in a broadcast watched by about 56.4 million viewers Back Earth.

If Navya didn't return, Marijus would be expected to pair off with someone else—for the good of the colony. Navya was willing to bet good oxygen that Gwyneth Lloyds would make a play for him. Navya felt her lip curl in a sneer. Gwyneth hadn't even been born on Mars; she had come fifteen years back on the ship dubbed "Noah's Ark" by the media, for all of the many new supplies brought to help the colony expand past the very basics, including whole families.

Navya hadn't liked Gwyneth since the day she'd been told she would be expected to share her toys with the little brat, just because they were close in age. She had tried to explain the *enormous* difference between her six and Gwyneth's five, but the grownups hadn't listened. When there were only a handful of children ranging in age from infancy to preteen, such niceties were ignored—for the good of the colony.

Navya was struck by a horrifying thought: What if she was reincarnated as a child of Marijus and Gwyneth? She didn't believe in reincarnation, of course, not really, but odds were good that if she died, the next baby conceived would be the child of Gwyneth and Marijus, and even with everything her parents had left behind Back Earth, a few beliefs still lingered.

The press release to be sent with her wedding photos talked up the fact that she came from a Hindu background and Marijus came from a Muslim background, as if they had personally set aside differences that were still issues Back Earth, rather than being raised in a scientific community that understood no amount of prayer would fix a faulty oxygen purifier. They both ate Petri pork without giving it a second thought, but the press release made them sound almost like star-crossed lovers.

Doing something for the good of the colony was fine, but at the moment Navya was mad at her ancestors for inventing that damned *maangtikka*—the head jewelry all Hindi brides were expected to wear. In the process of being flipped upside-down several times by the storm, it had come lose from her hair, fallen down through the suit and managed to wedge itself into her bra. The hock that was supposed to keep it attached to her hair was poking her left breast. It had been in her mother's family for generations, and her mother, in an uncharacteristic fit of sentimentality, had used up part of her precious weight allotment to bring it to Mars.

As Navya had been preparing for the wedding, her mother had tried to explain traditions she herself only vaguely recalled learning. Navya thought it sounded like the bride was handed over to the groom's family as if the bride's family couldn't wait to get rid of her. Still, she had agreed to the headgear, because it would look good in the photo shoot, and it would make a good "something old."

113

The fact that her regular bio-suit boots were her "something blue" had probably saved her life. The Vera Wang creation came with a set of boots that had high heels, pointy toes, and a loose attachment that had to constantly be fixed with heat tape. If she had been wearing them now, she would either be making much, much slower progress in the constrictive footgear, or outright dead from exposure, since the sandstorm probably would have managed to rip them off.

Still, even with boots that fit her own feet, they didn't fit with the rest of the suit, and even with the heat tape to create a proper seal, a small amount of grit had worked its way in. A tiny clump of dust, including a tiny pebble, had worked its way to the bottom of her left boot, and was rubbing up against her heel. Right now it was just annoying, but if she was stuck out here for too long, it was going to be yet another item of the list of Things That Could Kill Her.

She looked up at the setting sun and the thin clouds streaking across the sky. There was no sign of the turbulent havoc of the morning. The way ahead stretched on and on. By now everything was probably back to normal at the colony. Once the sandstorm had passed everyone would have gone straight to work repairing damage and performing a sweep of the solar panels to ensure they were able to keep collecting sunlight.

Any search and rescue operation would be perfunctory at best. No one had survived the heart of a sandstorm before. And, she cynically reminded herself, that might still be true if the ordeal managed to kill her in the end.

Navya saw something on the horizon. She squinted. Raising her hand to shield her eyes, she strained to see, hoping her brain wasn't supplying a visage of false hope. She decided now was a time to expend energy and took several leaps to cover more ground quickly. She looked again. There on the horizon were tiny, artificial straight lines that could only be the bank of windmills just outside the colony. Her heart gave a lurch. She was going to make it home.

Her foot caught on something, and she went sprawling.

Well, as long as she didn't do something stupid, like forget to look where she was going, she berated herself. It would be so *embarrassing* if her corpse was found just outside the colony. Carefully, she picked herself up and began moving forward again, faster now. The sun was setting, and the temperature was plummeting.

She lengthened her stride, feeling the cold begin to creep in, despite the warmth of her sweat. After what felt like no time at all the sun slipped below the horizon. She was running now, keeping one eye on the glint of metal ahead of her, another eye on where her feet landed. The suit began to make alarmed beeping noises at her for an excess of oxygen consumption.

As the light dimmed, she forced herself to slow down. She had to find a way to keep her bearings. In the dark it would be easy to walk in a wide circle and fall down a crevice, thinking she was still headed straight towards the colony.

She stopped, listened, frowned, listened harder. She could hear bagpipes in the wind. It was the familiar whining moan of "Amazing Grace." Oh no, she thought, someone must have died. With a gasp she realized she had arrived home in time for her own funeral.

Following the song, she managed to make her way to the colony. At the front door she tapped in the security code that would unlock the main entrance. Her fingers shook as she punched in the numbers. She stepped into the first airlock. Because she was a colonist with the proper opening sequence, and not a sandstorm or meteorite trying to batter down the door, there were no alarms at the opening of the airlocks or the main entrance. Another code let her into the colony proper. Fumbling, she undid the neck clasps and tugged off the helmet, gulping in the sweet, warm air. The bagpipes were louder now.

She thrust her hand down her front to wrench out the maangtikka and had to remind herself that ancient jewelry shouldn't be thrown against walls. Clenching it tightly in one fist, she limped through empty hallways, following the sound of the bagpipes.

She got to the door to the Main Hall just as the song was finishing. She opened the door on the final note and felt as though she had stepped, note perfect, into a performance. Dr. Joseph Harrington-Murphy was dragging out the last mournful note, and all heads were bowed. At the sound of the door opening, all heads snapped up in shock, and the astrophysicist nearly dropped his bagpipes.

Later, when she was rehydrated and refreshed, she would reflect on how satisfying it was to see that she had been genuinely mourned by the whole community, but right at the moment, standing in the front of the crowd, all she thought was that she *really* didn't like the way Gwyneth had her arm around Marijus.

She walked into the silent crowd, ignoring how much her foot hurt as she forced herself to make the last few steps. On the side she could see a table set up with most of the food she herself had helped prepare for her wedding. It was only practical, of course, but she couldn't suppress a snort of irritation at how fast her life was being recycled. She saw that someone had performed some primitive surgery to the cake to try and rework the cheerful dessert into something more somber for the occasion.

Dr. Anita Sakai had lit one of her precious sandalwood incense sticks. "Death sticks," the children called them, since she most often lit them for funerals, and everyone equated that spicy smell with the passing of another colonist.

116

As Navya walked, she ignored the wails of joy and bursts of questions that began popping up around her.

"My baby!" gasped her mother. She sobbed again, "My baby!" Pratibha Patel slumped against her younger daughter Jiya, continuing to sob, as Jiya looked back and forth with wide eyes, unsure whether to be more shocked by her big sister's miraculous reappearance or their normally stoic mother's hysterical outburst. Jiya was forced to concentrate on their mother, struggling to keep her upright.

Captain Stang, well known for his atheism, swore, "Jesus Christ! It's a God damned miracle!"

Marijus stared at her, his blood shot eyes wide with disbelief to see an actual miracle come true. "Navya," he whispered, a lifetime of love and longing in one word.

She ignored that as well, although it was gratifying to hear. She kept moving forward, ignoring the hands pressing against her to help.

She finished her trek, face to face with Gwyneth.

"Get. Off."

Gwyneth scurried away, and Navya clamped her arm around Marijus. "Let's get married," she told him. It came out in a hoarse growl.

As people converged around them, she asked for some of the Phobos-shine that was being passed around, but the medical staff insisted on a saline drip instead. Still, against medical advice, bandaged up and determined, she was standing next to Marijus as they said their vows to Captain Stang within the hour.

After the brief ceremony, she sat right back down and was content to prop her foot up, as Marijus sat next to her, holding her hand, touching her back, kissing her, or dashing over to the buffet table to bring as much food and drink as she wanted. She tapped her good foot to music and sipped her drink. Tomorrow, it would be back to work, for the good of the colony, but for now, she was going to enjoy the party.

A little over a century later, Kasei Sarabhai, Navya's great-great-granddaughter, proudly walked down the aisle in Zhulong City with a small pebble in her shoe, as all brides did on Mars, proud to limp ever forward.

About the Author

Kara Race-Moore has been fascinated by what life might be like on other planets ever since being introduced to Anne McCaffrey's dragon-riding heroines. Ms. Race-Moore lives in Massachusetts and works in educational publishing.

*****~~~~*****

The Read Planet

by Chuck Rothman

He awoke—and wanted Mars. And John Carter always got what he wanted.

He had thought about Mars for 47 years, ever since he had stumbled upon Edgar Rice Burroughs. It was heady stuff for a 12-year-old boy, and he had devoured each installment of the saga. He had even started calling himself John instead of the "Giovanni" that was on his birth certificate. His grandfather, who had given him the dog-eared and yellowing paperback, didn't mind that his grandson had forsaken his name. "Mars fits you," he said.

But today, it was different. It was within reach.

Carter undid the netting. He had grown used to sleeping without gravity, and, at his age, was grateful to wake up without the aches and pains of the Earth pulling him to the mattress. He swam through the air to the port. He had insisted on a real window, not a video. He wanted to see the planet directly.

The planet filled the port, its rough and ruddy surface begging him to visit. It had been growing each day, but now would get no larger. The *Bradbury* was in orbit, and soon its crew would be setting foot on the surface.

And he would be part of it. Not the first one down—he didn't need the fame—but part of the crew, the one string attached when he donated nearly half the money needed to get there.

"I should have come sooner," he muttered. It was a foolish conceit. Mars had been cold and dusty for eons, but Carter had always believed—first jokingly, then later so seriously that he never discussed the subject—that the Mars probes had ruined the planet. Before NASA went looking, Mars was a place of magic, of Red and Green

Martians fighting over a princess, and of the thousand versions of Martian life that he had devoured in his reading. The facts were dull and barren, missing the things that made that little red disk in the sky a beacon calling to him.

But he didn't mourn the loss. Not now, with Mars floating above the ship like a ripe apple ready for picking.

"And I shouldn't be daydreaming," he told himself. He had to get ready.

He pushed off the wall, and felt the pain in his chest.

It was different from the dull tightness he'd been keeping secret for several weeks. This was a sledgehammer pounding into his heart, crushing it with cold malice.

"No," he whispered. He tried to think, but he could only contemplate the pain and what it meant.

He could tough it out. It was just an overreaction to a pulled muscle in his chest. At his age, that wasn't surprising.

The pounding continued, radiating outward.

He had kept his motion and was heading for the open doorway. He dimly knew he had to stop himself, so no one else could see his weakness. Grabbing at the doorframe, he held on.

"Carter?"

It was Virginia Landis, the last person he wanted to see right then. "What's the matter?" she asked.

He tried to shake her off. "Nothing. A little indigestion." He felt like he was going to vomit.

She grabbed his wrist and quickly took a pulse. "My God," she whispered, then she let go abruptly. "Don't move. I'm going to get my EMT kit."

"That's not necessary," he grunted, his teeth clenched to fight the pain. It wasn't helping.

His vision blurred. "Damn," he said. He felt lightheaded, and it was hard to think. "Mars," he whispered just before he blacked out.

...

When Carter awoke, he was zipped into his sleep netting. For a moment, he dared to think it had been just a dream, but the dull ache in his chest told him otherwise.

Landis was hovering nearby. "How are you feeling?"

He forced a smile. "Great!" he said. "I don't know what hit me, but I bet it scared the hell out of you." He reached to unzip the net. "When do we leave?" he asked.

Landis shook her head. "Don't say, 'we.' You're staying here."

"It was just a little indigestion."

"You know better than that. More importantly, *I* know better than that. It was a heart attack."

"I'm fine," Carter said. He sat up and tried to loosen himself. His hands felt clumsy, and the small exertion of moving drained him.

"You most definitely are not. I don't even know if you'll get back to Earth alive."

The hell with Earth. "Damn it, do something! Fix this."

"There's only one thing that might help. A bypass."

"Then do that."

"Right. In microgravity without an operating room or equipment. Not to mention the fact I've never done any surgery in my life." She shook her head. "No, Carter. You may die of this, but I'm not going to kill you."

"Now, wait just a minute. . . "

"No. *You* wait." Her eyes were tight and filled with fury. "How long have you been keeping this secret? When did you have your last attack?"

He fell silent. She had guessed, but he wasn't going to give her the satisfaction of knowing it. "Virginia," he said quietly, "I plan to be on the *Ylla*."

"I won't let you. You've endangered—" She paused. "I'm sorry," she said. "I know this is disappointing, but you won't survive the landing."

"I've survived worse. If I don't make it, it's not your fault." He held up his hand. "I absolve you of all blame," he said in his most serious voice, like a priest in a confessional. He grinned. "That better?"

"This is no joking matter."

"I'm *not* joking." He tried again. His motions were slow and deliberate, but he was able to loosen the net and float free. "I need to go down. I need to walk on Mars."

"Why?"

He realized he could not articulate an answer. It had been a part of him for so many decades that he never asked himself the question. Should he tell her he got all sentimental because of a few cheesy stories when he was a kid? Hell, he hadn't looked at the Burroughs books in years, afraid he'd see through their clumsy style and lose his dream. Because he was a dreamer?

Of course not. They called him "Knife-in-the-Back" Carter, making money in any way he could. He thought of himself more like Burroughs's John Carter, swinging a sword, leaping high, and not afraid to be ruthless when it was necessary. He had taken his father's small fortune and turned it into a big one, with a single-mindedness that had frightened a lot of his associates.

No one would believe he was a dreamer. And no one understood why he had suddenly put his fortune into the nearly defunct Mars project.

There was no way to explain it all now. "Why?" he finally said. "Because it's there. That was good enough for Mallory."

"Mallory?"

"Mountain climber. Died while trying to scale Everest."

"I doubt Mallory died of a heart attack," Landis said.

"It doesn't matter. I didn't come all this way just to look at Mars through my window." He glanced out, to reassure himself; the planet still was there, silent and ready. He wanted it.

She took his arm and said, "I'm afraid that's just the way it works out."

...

Several times Carter tried to free himself from his flimsy prison, only to be stopped by his weakness. He could hear the talk down the hall, the voices barely recognizable. But he knew what they were saying. There were a few—like Ransom, the commander—who didn't want him along in the first place.

But he never would have gotten all this way if he gave up easily. He rested, gathering his strength, one eye on the clock.

The *Ylla* would be launching soon. It would not leave without him.

Carefully, he unzipped the netting.

He felt better, though he didn't know how much exertion he could manage. He would just have to find out.

The main corridor was empty. He could hear the voices to his left, the other crew members going over what needed to be done to prepare. Good.

The *Ylla* was near the stern. He pulled himself along, slowly but steadily, conserving his strength. He felt his heart racing, though he had no idea if this was just excitement, or something more dangerous.

Ahead of him, in one of the supply rooms, he heard voices. He moved forward cautiously, and, just as he was reaching the open door, he recognized Ransom.

The commander did not sound pleased. "I knew we shouldn't have brought him along."

"He's dying." It was Landis, the words gentle in tone, but harsh in their rebuke.

There was a pause. "I'm sorry for the old bastard, but he shouldn't be here."

Carter glanced in. He was in luck; their backs were to him. They were so involved in their discussion that he was able to slip past. Finally, he reached the ready room. No one was behind him. Good.

There were six suits on the walls. One for everyone. That had been part of the plan—no one would stay behind.

He found his suit. It was larger than the others, designed for his older body.

If I'm already there and strapped in, he thought, they'll find it hard to get me out.

The work was difficult. The pants just wouldn't behave; he had to go through contortions to get his feet in place. By the time he snapped on his boots, he was breathing raggedly.

But there was no pain. He held on to that thought.

The top came next. It was difficult to get the zippers lined up, and his fingers didn't want to move the way they needed to. So, through agonizing progress, he worked with what he had.

"Look at you."

Carter looked up. Landis was watching his struggle. He turned away, wanting to be done before she stopped him.

"You can barely breathe. Are you feeling dizzy, too?"

"A little," Carter said. He zipped up the front of his suit and turned for the helmet.

Landis held it. "You can't go, Carter. I won't let you."

"You can't stop me," he said, but knew the words rang hollow.

"You got us here," she said. "You have to be satisfied with that."

Carter laughed. "Satisfied? Do you think I'd ever settle for *satisfied*? I want Mars. It's all that really means anything to me."

124

"Oh, stop being so dramatic," she said crossly. "You have your businesses, your family."

"I sold my businesses, remember? As for my family, my wife is dead, and my children tried to have me committed for doing this. Right now, I only have Mars."

Landis shook her head sadly. "I know how much you want Mars. But you're not going to get it. Now get out of that suit and back to your bed."

He knew better than anyone else what determination was, and he could hear the determination in her voice as she spoke. He had lost, lost the real Mars as surely as he had lost the Mars of his youth.

But there was something in her words, something she had not yet come to realize.

"No," he said, understanding. "I'm going to land."

"It *will* kill you."

He felt some of his strength returning. He was on top of the situation now. "Maybe. But I could also die if I stay. And *that's* why you're going to let me aboard."

"What are you talking about?"

"You feel responsible for me. Which means you wouldn't leave me alone on the *Bradbury*. It would eat at your conscience if I died while you were gone. So you'll have to stay up here with me."

"You don't know what you're talking about. You'll be safe and stable up here."

He could see from the abrupt way she moved as she spoke that she was trying to deny what he knew was true. "No. You wouldn't leave me. You might not think so now, but when the time comes, you're going to stay on the *Bradbury* and watch the others walk on Mars. And you'll hate that, because you want Mars as much as I do."

Landis didn't answer.

Carter knew she needed a push. "You asked me a question before. I didn't know the answer myself until now. You asked me 'why?' I came here for one reason—to search for Barsoom."

125

She looked blank. "What?"

"Barsoom. Or Malacandra. Or even 'A Martian Odyssey.' They're stories. Visions of Mars. Barsoom had men with different colored skins fighting each other with swords and spears, all over the princess Dejah Thoris. Silly stuff, really, but you don't think that when you're reading it. I read it as a kid, and I knew I had to have Mars."

"Those are just books," Landis said.

"So? Without those books, we wouldn't be here. Why do you think the ship's named the *Bradbury?* Books made us want Mars. *I* wanted Mars. And, by God, I'm going to get it."

"You'll die."

"Then let me die trying!" His pulse was racing, but he felt no pain. He managed to calm down. "Which leads me to a question. The same one you asked me. Why?"

She seemed as hesitant as he had been when pressed. After a moment, she said, "To add to human scientific knowledge."

"Bullshit," said Carter. "You could have done that on Earth. Watch monkeys in Madagascar. What made you choose Mars?"

She stood, her body stiff, as though wishing he'd drop the subject.

"A book?" he said softly.

She sighed. "An article. It was in an old science fiction magazine my mother was throwing out. It said there was water on Mars, and that meant life. Bacteria, I think. It. . . thrilled me. I decided I wanted to go there."

Carter nodded. "Something you read. So you see? We're not that different. *What* we read was different, but the words brought us here. They captured you, just like they captured me and everyone else here." He paused. "I don't want to deny you Mars. Don't deny it to me."

She fell silent. Carter didn't know if that was a good or bad sign. He waited. "You'll die on the way down," she said.

Carter laughed, giddy. "Never. Even if my heart stops, I'll still keep moving just long enough to feel that Martian dust under my boots."

Landis grinned. "Oh, hell," she said. "Let me help you with your suit."

...

The roar of the rockets came to a halt. An even louder silence filled the cabin of the *Ylla.* All eyes were on Carter.

He didn't move.

The silence grew dangerous, almost a living thing that no one wanted to disturb. Finally, Landis spoke. "Carter?" she asked.

Carter opened his eyes. "It's all right," he said. "Everything is all right."

"Any pain?"

Carter shook his head. Easier to do that then tell a lie. His chest felt like the gee forces had never stopped. He could only breathe shallowly, hoping it would ease things. If it did any good, he didn't notice.

But he was on Mars.

"Here," Landis said. "Let me help you up."

He shook her off. "I can manage. I want to get there without help."

It was a struggle. He felt too weak to move. He was dying, he knew. But not here, encased in this metal can. He stood up. His heart was racing, and he paused to catch his breath.

And he realized everyone was looking at him. "Go on," he said. "You have a planet to explore."

Ransom looked at Landis, then at Carter. "We kind of thought you'd be the first one down."

"What? Why?"

"Because you wanted it more than anyone else."

Carter didn't know what to say. And there was usually only one thing in those sorts of circumstances.

"Thank you."

He had trouble unbuckling from the chair. His hands were weak, and his fingers couldn't get the hang of the movements.

Landis looked over and began to reach for the buckles.

Carter shook his head. No help. Not until there was no other choice.

Finally, the buckle released.

Carter stood up. The movement made him dizzy, but he didn't let it stop him. He walked, carefully but firmly, to the door.

A tiny camera, sending images back to Earth, followed his every move.

Carter gave a wave, then stepped into the airlock.

The weight on his chest was as crushing as ever. He gasped as the airlock cycled.

The door opened.

It was a vast reddish desert, dunes of ancient rock stretching as far as the eye could see. In the distance, eroded mountains of browns and reds and yellows crouched, like a New England hillside in the autumn. It was the most beautiful sight he had ever seen. "God," he whispered, overcome, as the pressure in his chest became nearly unbearable. "God, we made it!"

He could say no more. The air in his suit seemed thinner than the Martian atmosphere. His head felt light, and he began to waver.

Then, just before he thought he would collapse, the pain vanished. The episode was past, and he could see clearly.

Dejah Thoris stood before him, standing in the green of the ancient seabed. She smiled as she saw him. "Welcome back to Barsoom, John Carter," she said.

The Read Planet

"My princess," Carter said, and knew he had come home.

About the Author

Chuck Rothman has been writing and publishing science fiction for over 30 years, with stories in *Asimov's Science Fiction, Fantasy and Science Fiction, Baen's Universe, Strange Horizons, Penumbra*, and *Daily SF,* plus in the anthologies *Unidentified Funny Objects* and *Futuredaze.* His two novels, *Staroamer's Fate* and *Syron's Fate,* were recently republished by Fantastic Books. He lives in Schenectady, New York.

*****~~~~*****

Photo and Art Credits and Acknowledgments

Make Carrots, Not War - Carrots of many colors, Wikipedia Commons

Colorblind on the Red Planet - Mars Exploration Program - Mars as Art: "Martian Mosaic" (http://mars.nasa.gov/multimedia/marsasart/?s=26)

The Canary and the Roach - giant burrowing cockroach image from Australianmuseum.net.au

The FALCON - Humans explore an area called Noctis Labyrinthus, located in the Valles Marineris system of enormous canyons. Image by Pat Rawlings, courtesy of NASA

First Step - Photo detail of Cydonia region on Mars with the optical illusion "Face on Mars." 1976 NASA Viking mission.

Cover Design - Keely Rew

Readers - Andrew Cairns, Tom Parker, and Keely Rew

*****~~~~~*****

Discover other titles by Third Flatiron:

(1) Over the Brink: Tales of Environmental Disaster

(2) A High Shrill Thump: War Stories

(3) Origins: Colliding Causalities

(4) Universe Horribilis

(5) Playing with Fire

(6) Lost Worlds, Retraced

THIRD FLATIRON